THE OVERLOOKED

SIMON ORÉ MOLINA

with illustrations by
ROMAN DIRGE

ERASERHEAD PRESS
PORTLAND, OREGON

ERASERHEAD PRESS
833 SE Main St. #342
Portland, OR 97214

www.eraserheadpress.com

ISBN: 9781621053286
Copyright © 2023 by Simon Oré Molina
Cover art copyright © 2023 Rafael Gandine
Interior art copyright © 2023 Roman Dirge
Cover and interior design by Rose O'Keefe

Printed in the USA.

THE
OVERLOOKED

A Book For Strange Grownups, About Two
Little Girls Who Live At The Overlook Hotel.

For Stephen and Stanley.

With apologies to both.

THANK YOU!

Stephen King, Stanley Kubrick, Carlton Mellick III, Rose O'Keefe, Duke Johnson, James Fino, Casey Rup, Ross Clark, Tish Burns, Mary Blakemore, Mariana Da Silva, Lupita Molina, Cameron Pierce, Christopher Rullan, Maïa Oré-Rullan, Santiago "Littleface" Rullan, Patricia Molina, Bob Oré, Lupita Basteris de Molina, Enrique Molina & Tom Mendoza

And an extra special thank you to Hellen & Celia "Teddy" Smith, for letting me borrow your names

"Are you sure you wouldn't like to run? A game of tag, perhaps? All we have is time, you know. An eternity of time."
Stephen King, *The Shining*

PROLOGUE

Hellen and Teddy are two little girls who live in a big hotel far away from town called The Overlook. The Overlook, like most fancy hotels, has many floors filled with tastefully decorated rooms. It has mirrored hallways, a grand staircase, and floors carpeted in beautiful, hypnotic patterns. It also has something that most hotels do not, and that is a large elaborate hedge maze in the garden.

When guests aren't around, like right now, when it is covered in a thick white blanket of cold and the hotel is closed to living guests, the garden labyrinth is one of the girls' favorite places to play. Teddy especially loves playing with the topiary animals that surround the maze. Teddy also loves it when they trim the topiary animals, or what she calls 'giving them a haircut'. *SNIP SNIP SNIP!* The hedge scissors sing as they trim the leaves! Teddy loves watching the gardeners find the animals hiding within the hedges. She likes to imagine that creatures are being freed from leafy cocoons. Hellen doesn't like the hedge maze animals because there are no hedge sharks, only hedge lions, and hedge snakes, and hedge elephants. Hellen loves sharks and thinks they are the best animal. Much better than spiders. There is a playground beyond the hedge maze. Two slides, a big swing set with half a dozen swings, a jungle gym, a tunnel made of cement rings, a sandbox, and a playhouse that is an exact replica of The Overlook itself. But that winter it had been avalanched by snow and was not an option for the girls to play with.

Beyond the snow-covered swing sets, there was a long and cobblestoned drive that led up to the hotel. The girls are permanent residents of The Overlook, along with their Mother and Father and the rest of the hotel staff. There are also guests of the hotel that, like Hellen and Teddy, can never leave and are there year-round. Oh, that's right children, Teddy and Hellen, and most of the people in this story, are already dead and have been so for quite a bit of time.

Even though their mother comes by every night to tuck them in and tell them a bedtime story, they hardly see their parents. Not since Dad got angry and chopped Hellen and Teddy up into pieces with an axe. *CHOP CHOP CHOP*. Ever since then, Hellen and Teddy can't leave the hotel, or change their clothes, or ever get older. They stay the same ages, 8 and 6. Their mother insists that even though they are free to roam about the hotel during the daytime, and during off-season, they are strictly prohibited from talking or playing with the living guests, and from being out in the hotel after bedtime. Which, their mother would tell them, is every day at sundown, on the dot. Teddy doesn't think much of their curfew but Hellen believes after dark is when their father, Mr. Grady, would be wandering the halls. She has no proof of this, of course, because even though they know their father is in the hotel somewhere, they haven't seen him in a very long time.

Everyone thinks the girls are twins, but Hellen is two full years older than Teddy. However, Hellen is very small for her age and the fact that their mother dressed them in similar dresses before they died, makes it even harder to tell that they are just sisters. Teddy liked it that people thought she was Hellen's twin, but Hellen finds it insulting. Hellen liked to list the many ways Teddy and her were different. "I like sharks because they are ruthless if you bother them, but cool if you leave them alone. Like me." Hellen would tell Mr. Braddock, the concierge of The Overlook Hotel. "Teddy likes spiders. She saves them and keeps them as pets."

"How interesting" Mr. Braddock would say. He, like most adults, didn't really listen to children when they spoke. Mr. Braddock died in the hotel a long time ago, but has never told the girls how he died, even though they have asked him that question several times. Hellen is pretty sure it has to do with the stab wound in his belly, which is always leaving a blood stain on his shirt in the shape of a crooked smile.

"And Teddy likes to climb things, like trees and lamps and couches. But I like to go to the library and read books about pirates and kings and stories about romance and not climb on the shelves like a monkey when I do! You see? We're like night and day, how can people think we are twins?" Hellen kicked at the front desk trying to keep Mr. Braddock's attention.

"Yes, I see." Said Mr. Braddock. But Hellen could tell he was more occupied with arranging the keys to the rooms on their little hooks than listening to her list the ways she and Teddy were not twins.

Every morning Mr. Braddock took all the keys for all the doors in the hotel off their hooks and mixed them up in a box so they got all jumbled up. Then he spent the rest of the day placing the right key back on its appropriate hook. He never looked satisfied when he did this, he always had a bored look on his face, as if this was an eternal punishment. Teddy thought it was a little funny, but Hellen thought it was a little sad. This is another way in which the two are different.

Every night before Hellen and Teddy go to sleep, their mother comes to visit them and tells them a bedtime story.

Their mother always starts the story the same way:

"Once upon a time there were two little blackbirds that were the best of friends. And the two little birds would fly around the sky and laugh and sing and play games. The little blackbirds lived in a cozy nest made out of an old hand basket in the tippy-top branch of an aspen tree that overlooked the garden.

It was there, in that nest, that they looked out at the sky and saw two older birds struggle to fly against the cold, harsh wind. The younger of the two little blackbirds laughed at the older birds, "We are much stronger than them," she said, "we have no problem flying against such gusts!" But the other little blackbird remarked that one day they too would be older birds, and struggle against the wind. The first bird asked her friend if they would still be able to play together, like they did now, even when they became older birds. Even if the winds became too much for them, could they still play? The second bird looked at her friend and shook her head sadly, she told the younger bird that even though they would play together now, as time went by, they would fly in different directions, they would grow up and grow apart.

And so the little birds became sad. One of them wondered then, what if they were to make a wish? A wish that they could stay young forever! Be beautiful little blackbirds and play for as long as they'd like. The younger blackbird loved that idea and so they set off to find the wishing rock that was hidden away in the forest..."

The story would go on from there, telling the tale of the little birds as they went searching for the wishing rock. Sometimes they would meet a giant that would help them look, other times they would outsmart a snake that was trying to eat them. Every time the adventure would change a little, but the ending was always the same.

"When the little blackbirds at last found the wishing rock, they fluttered around in great excitement. They asked

the rock to be able to remain young and play together always and forever. The rock heard their wish and knew it was pure, for young little blackbirds are always good at heart, and it was then that the magical woodsman came out of the woods with his enchanted wand. He went to the little birds and whacked their little heads and wings with the magic stick, Whack whack whack, *and just like that, the spell was cast. The little birds would remain young and could return to their nest to play forever and ever and ever."*

After she would tell them the story, their mommy would kiss them goodnight. She would always close the curtain shut and make sure to tuck her little blackbirds in tight. It was the only part of the day when they spent any time with their mother.

Hellen would sometimes draw a picture of her and her mommy together, with her crayons. Sometimes she'd put Teddy in the drawing and sometimes she wouldn't. Hellen would slip the drawing under the bathroom door in her mother's room, in an attempt to cheer her mother up, but she never said anything to Hellen about them, nor would she respond in any way when Hellen slipped the drawings to her via the crack at the bottom of the bathroom door. Teddy would compliment Hellen on how pretty the bullet hole in mommy's face looked, in the drawings.

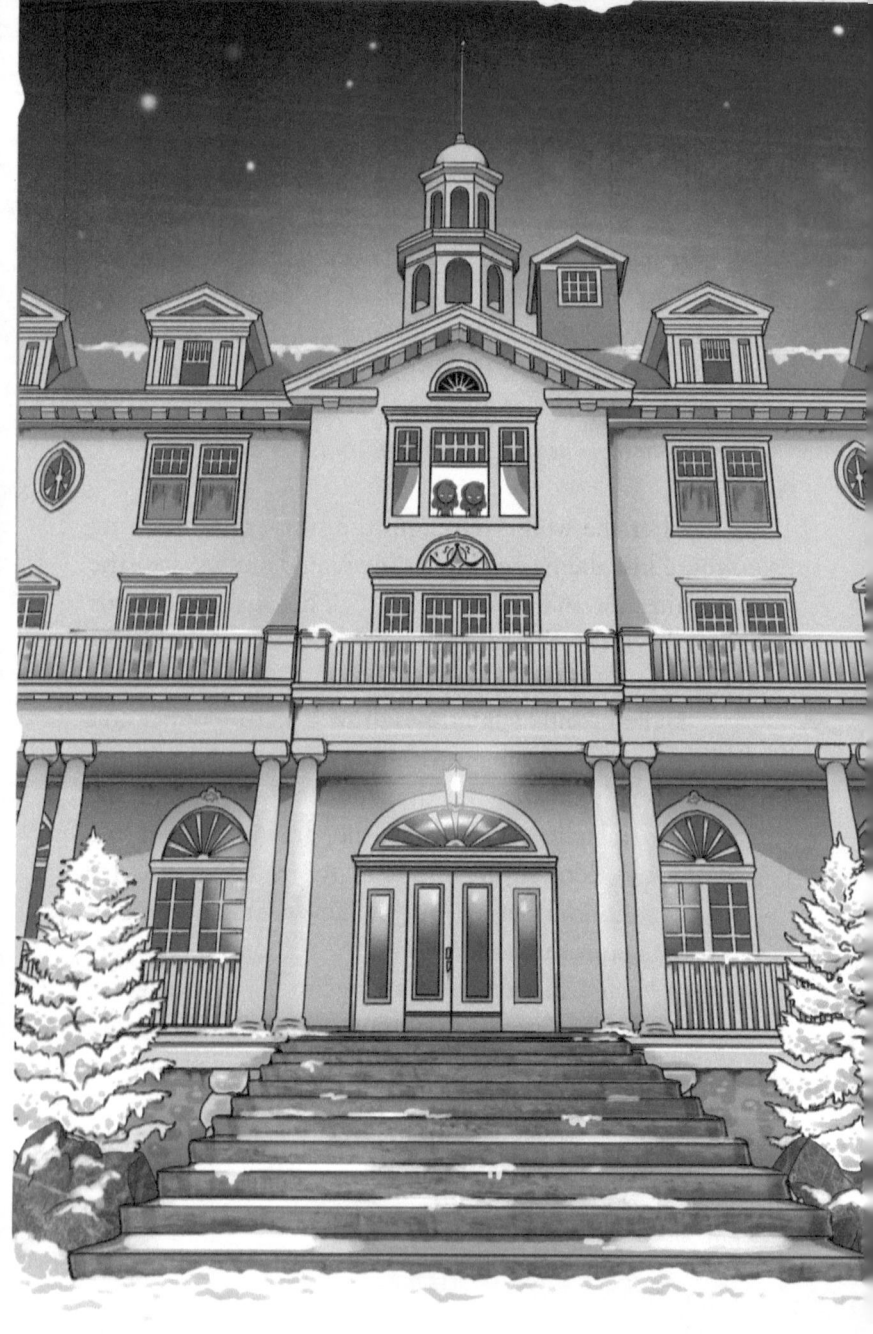

CHAPTER
ONE

Hellen and Teddy were in their bedroom, which was located on the tippy top floor of The Overlook Hotel, perched high and with a view of the snow-covered grounds. It was wintertime at The Overlook and that meant the hotel had no guests.

Usually, Hellen and Teddy would wake up on winter mornings and take the elevator straight down to the kitchen so Cook could make them breakfast. Even though the girls are ghosts, they still need a proper breakfast to start the day off right!

But on this day, Hellen was distracted. On this day Hellen hadn't been able to sleep the night before, something she had seen *or thought she had seen* had kept her awake.

Finding herself quite unable to fall into that deep state of rest that ghosts called sleep, she took the initiative to wander about the giant mess of a hotel in search of the best place to watch the sunrise and think.

There had been someone new at the hotel the other day, she was sure of it, *or was she?*, a little boy that was playing and then suddenly disappeared before Hellen could talk to him.

The image of his cute little face was burned into Hellen's mind, like a branding iron on the flesh of a cow. She had seen him a few times now, once playing on the carpet and another time through the impossible window in the general manager's office, running towards the playground outside.

That's where Hellen found herself as the sun rose above the massive rooftop of the hotel, which looked like frosted oatmeal cookies, with the dusting of fine white snow that sat on the dark brown shingles.

Hellen was staring at the replica of The Overlook that sat in the center of the playground. The detail in the miniature hotel was impressive. But it wasn't totally accurate—as Hellen knew all too well, the hotel was very different on the inside than it was on the outside.

As she looked over the tiny hedge maze and topiary models, she noticed something out of place. It was a dead spider, taken by the cold. The spider's legs curled and snow-covered, looked like a petals of a wilting flower made out of coat-hanger wire. And maybe it was because it looked like a wilting flower that Hellen picked it up and took it back to her room, on the tippy top floor, of The Overlook Hotel.

Hellen was standing against the corner of her bedroom with her nose right up against where the walls meet. She inhaled deeply as she talked to herself.

"He loves me, he loves me not" Hellen whispered and plucked the legs off of the frozen spider. The sound the legs made when they snapped off was like the sound you made by biting into frozen snow peas.

When Teddy noticed what Hellen was doing she gave out a blood-curdling shriek! Do you know what that sounds like children? Well, it is just an awful sound, like a rusty nail banging around a tea kettle that is past its boiling point. And that shriek snapped Hellen right out of her daydream.

"What are you doing to my spider!!?" Teddy screamed.

"Relax, you nerd, this one was already dead. I found it outside in the snow. It didn't come from your collection." Hellen said the word *collection* in a way that suggested she didn't like spiders the same way her sister did.

Teddy calmed down a little and ran over to her closet where she kept all her pet spiders. She called them out by name as she counted.

"There's Snow and Rose and Mary and Bacon. There's Ghostpepper and Kingsley and Maïa and Mellick. And of course Buckle and Pugsley. Okay, they're all here," she sighed in relief.

"I told you. Don't be such a baby." Hellen picked up the discarded spider legs off the floor, having lost her count.

"I'm not a baby," Teddy complained. "I'm just as tall as you are."

"I'm still *two* years older than you and you shouldn't forget that."

"What were you doing with that spider, by the way?" Teddy asked her sister, adding for good measure, "And you're sure it was dead before you started pulling its legs off?"

"Yes," Hellen said, rolling her eyes a little. "I wouldn't lie about something like that. I know you love these icky things."

"They aren't icky," smiled Teddy. "They are very useful and wonderful things. They eat up all the gross bugs and make cool sticky webs with their assholes. They are awesome! Don't avoid the question."

Hellen didn't want to lie to her little sister, but she also didn't want to tell her what she was doing with that dead spider, because it was a secret and she was a little embarrassed about it. She was in a difficult situation. And so Hellen decided to tell the truth, but not the whole truth.

"I was asking the spider a question."

"What were you asking a dead spider?" Teddy asked with a furrowed brow.

"I was asking it about something I saw the other day. I wanted to know something specific about the special thing I saw."

"What special thing did you see?" Teddy asked, getting tired of her sister dancing around the answer.

"Actually, I'm not even sure I saw him."

"*Him?*"

Hellen blushed and decided that this was enough talk about her spider, they hadn't even had their breakfast yet.

"Who is this him and why is him so special?" Teddy teased her sister.

"Let's get some food," Hellen said. "All this talk about spiders is making me hungry."

She tried to tease Teddy right back, but Teddy was already out the door and sprinting towards the elevator, while yelling back towards her sister, "Okay, but I'm not letting this go. You have to tell me your secret. No secrets between sisters!"

Hellen sighed, already regretting having told Teddy anything.

There was only one working elevator in The Overlook, which was silly since it was such a large hotel, but it seemed to be enough, and as far as the girls knew, the hotel only had one Elevator Operator and that was Otis.

Otis was very round and bursting at the seams like a bag of blood that had just a tiny bit more blood inside it than it should. Otis had tight skin that rippled if you touched it, like the top of a lake after you throw a pebble into it. Hellen was pretty sure Otis was very sick.

"Good morning, Otis," said Teddy, as she skipped inside the go-up-box, wedging herself into the elevator around what little room there was that wasn't being taken up by Otis.

"Good morning to you," Otis replied through his tiny mouth that looked like the knot on the bottom of a water balloon.

When the elevator got to the lobby, it made a creaky sound like an old woman getting out of a bathtub. It may have been a strange sound, but to the girls, it just meant that it was time to get out.

"Have a lovely day," the girls shouted to Otis the elevator operator as they ran down the lobby towards the kitchen.

"I'll surely try," answered Otis. And you could tell, if you looked at him say this, that he really did want to try and have a lovely day. But you could also tell that he didn't believe he ever would. The sadness in his eyes betrayed him every time. Do you know about that, children? About the sadness behind a person's eyes that gives away their true feelings? Well, if you don't, don't worry because you will. There will always be people with sadness behind their eyes.

CHAPTER
TWO

When Hellen and Teddy entered the kitchen, Cook was happy to see them. Cook was a very old lady who looked like she'd been a ghost for longer than anyone else at the hotel. Her skin appeared to have been beaten by whips and left to bleach in the sun after it was ripped from her body like a scab that hadn't quite healed. Her eyes were soft and gooey like those of a beautiful fish.

Teddy once asked her how old she was but Cook just smiled and said "I'm older than dirt but younger than mud." And she would laugh with her old lipless mouth. Oh yeah, Cook had a mouth with no lips, which made it very hard for her to speak, but Hellen and Teddy could always understand her.

"Oell ihitizzint teda Grady tins," said Cook.

"We're not twins!" Hellen complained, "I'm two full years older."

"Ah dat you aaa," Mumbled Cook.

"And as the older sister, I insist on picking today's breakfast." Hellen declared as Teddy sidled up to her and grabbed at her hand. Even though they were the same size, Teddy was still only 6, and though Teddy was by all accounts a braver and more self-assured person, she couldn't help but look up to Hellen.

Cook had a lot of things she loved to prepare for the ghostly guests of the hotel, but what she loved to cook up more than anything were maggots and rats and beetles. Her favorite thing to make was maggot pie with rat tail crust, or beetle ice cream with whipped worm purée. She would gobble them down in her lipless mouth like a hungry hungry hippo eating a cold corn-on-the-cob.

Hellen used to be fascinated with watching Cook eat, and would often stare at Cook, not really caring that it wasn't polite. It never seemed to bother Cook, and if it did, she never said anything about it. Cook had deep bruised scars on her mouth where her lips once were, Teddy thought this was because Cook must have eaten something really spicy one day and cut her own lips off in a hurry to stop the spice from spreading. Hellen thought it was probably someone who was angry with her that did it. The way their father chopped them up for making him angry. Hellen didn't tell Teddy this, because Teddy still had nice memories of their father, but all Hellen had in her heart for him was hate.

Teddy, on the other hand, did not like watching Cook eat at all! She thought it was way gross and cruel to eat rats and maggots. Cook would even admit that they didn't taste good, not nearly as good as real pies and ice cream did.

"Why do you eat them if they taste gross?" Teddy asked Cook one time.

"Oell Teddy-Air," Cook couldn't pronounce B's without any lips so she called Teddy *Teddy-Air* instead of *Teddy-Bear,* "it's cause when I died, my ody was eaten. Rats, aggots, orms, eetles - unching away at y flesh, niddle, niddle, niddle. They ate ee up. So now that I a ghost I like to eat the children of the easts that ate ee. If that akes sense." The girls nodded that it did.

"That," Cook told the girls, "is delicious irony." Although the girls weren't sure what irony meant, they smiled at Cook. No sense arguing with Cook before she'd made them breakfast. And it's none of that ironic breakfast for the girls today! Hellen and Teddy each had Cook get them a bowl of their favorite cereal, but instead of milk, the girls had Cook pour apple juice in their bowls. Hellen liked the combination because it made the cereal tart and bitter. Teddy liked it because she said it looked like someone took a piss in their breakfast and she thought that was hilarious. *Pissy Cereal*, she called it.

"What were you doing with that spider anyway?" Teddy asked her sister, with a mouthful of pissy cereal.

"Gross. Don't talk with your mouth full." Hellen brushed her sister's hand away.

"I'm going to find out eventually. I always do." Teddy tried to scoop up too much cereal into her mouth and it spilled all over the table, knocking over Hellen's bowl in the process. Teddy just laughed. Hellen rolled her eyes.

"Teddy, grow up!" But Teddy just laughed harder. She loved making her sister angry, because it meant Hellen was paying attention to her. Teddy loved it when Hellen paid attention to her.

"Tell me why you were hurting the spider and I'll stop bugging you."

"I wasn't hurting it, I told you it was already dead. I found it in the snow."

"When were you out in the snow?" Teddy asked, miming to Cook that she'd like more cereal please.

"I couldn't sleep yesterday night, something was keeping me up. Like something I was thinking about but didn't understand was keeping me up."

"I don't understand," Teddy said, confused.

"Exactly, so I opened the window to get some fresh air, not that we need it, being ghosts and all."

Teddy nodded, following Hellen's story.

"And I thought I saw something, something odd and so I snuck out the window onto the snowy ledge to get a better look. And that's when I saw him again."

"Saw who?"

"You're going to make fun of me."

"No, I won't," Teddy assured her.

"Promise not to tell anyone. And that includes Mommy." Teddy nodded.

"Well, there's a boy in the hotel. A new boy I've never seen before." Hellen whispered to Teddy so that Cook wouldn't hear.

"I don't think he's seen me yet, but I've seen him here and there. Just pop up, you know. I think he's close to our ages. And I don't know, I've been curious about him." Hellen was blushing when she spoke about him.

"I haven't seen any other kids here. Are you sure?"

"Teddy, I'm positive. He's a little blond boy, and he seems very sweet."

"Do you know his name?" Teddy asked as she ate another spoonful of apple juice soaked cheerios.

"Of course not. I haven't even met him yet, don't be silly." Hellen looked around to make sure no one else could hear them.

"But I've been calling him Santiago in my head." She smiled as she said his name.

"Santiago" Teddy sounded it out. "That's a silly name for an imaginary boyfriend."

"Teddy is a silly name for a baby. And he's not imaginary! And he's not my boyfriend! I never should have told you!"

"I'm sorry Hell." Teddy smiled, "I'm just poking fun. Where did you see *Santiago*? And why haven't we seen him before? I mean, wouldn't we know about another ghost kid in the hotel?" and before Hellen could say anything in response to all those logical questions Teddy slurped up her remaining pissy cereal and burped into Hellen's face.

"Why don't you ask Cook?" Teddy said, giggling. "She's been around a long, long, long time."

But Hellen didn't need to ask Cook. They hadn't been very discreet in talking about this mystery kid, and as a matter of fact, Cook had a feeling she could help.

Cook wobbled over to her old cookbooks and recipe cards. Long abandoned, since she'd memorized everything those books had to teach, the shelves were covered in grease stains and cobwebs. She pulled out an old wooden cigar box, with a faded pattern of red jugs marked xxx on the side. On the top of the box was a cartoon drawing of an old man with a long beard holding a bag of cherries and smoking a large cigar.

Cook explained that once, this box held a collection of the finest cigars she ever smoked, back when she had lips. They were Cherry Rum cigars. The tobacco leaves had been soaked in cherry-flavored dark rum that had been aged in oak barrels for years. Because of this, the rum and the tobacco leaves were tinted a light red and gave the smoke a taste of cherry honey.

It was amazing, but of course, Cook lamented, those cigars hadn't been made in a long time. Instead, the box was now filled with newspaper clippings of obituaries.

It was, Cook explained, her morbid collection of the death announcements of everyone who had died in the hotel. It was essentially a messy, deconstructed collage of The Overlook's ghost manifest. A list of all the dead people.

Cook and the girls went through each of the obituaries, over several bowls of pissy cereal, but found no one new. Every obituary was old and none of them mentioned anything about a young boy having died. It was a dead end.

"Here, you can have these clippings back," said Hellen as she collected them all in a pile, ready for the cigar box.

"It's okay, you can hang on to them," said Cook, "I think it's time I started a new collection. One that is less the past and more the future."

"Well, thank you for your help," Hellen said, as she stuffed the cut-up obituaries into the front pocket of her dress.

"What help? Her newspaper clippings were a dead end," Teddy told her sister.

"Still, it was nice of her to try," Hellen said.

With a good breakfast in their bellies, the Grady sisters decided to work together and solve the riddle of the mystery boy. Although Hellen swore he was real, Teddy was still not quite sure what to believe and so she suggested they ask Otis. Because if anyone would know if there was someone new in the hotel, it would be the elevator operator.

"Have you noticed any new people in the hotel this winter? Like any new families?" Hellen asked Otis.

"Sorry Miss Hellen, but I don't see much of anything outside of this go-up box."

"What do you mean? You go to every floor! You must see the rest of the hotel, you've got to be leaving the elevator to sleep and eat!"

"Sadly, I can't fit through the doors," Otis said with a jolly air of defeat.

"I'm far too big to live anywhere but inside the elevator. I used to be able to leave just like you and your twin sister. I would get invited to all the parties because I knew all the guests. And some of them would throw amazing and lavish get-togethers, that's what fancy grownups call shindigs, you see, and they would do blow and have key parties, which is what fancy grownups call cocaine and husband swapping sex orgies, and I would try to keep up, you see.

"I didn't feel like I fit in with that crowd and I thought that if I outdid them at the stuff they liked, if I ate more than them, if I drank more than them, I would win their respect. And that I wouldn't just be the guy in the elevator who could find drugs for them, but I would *be* one of them. You know?

"So I just kept drinking and eating and getting bigger and bigger. Like a balloon. And maybe it was the drugs, but it feels like no matter what I put into my body, it all turns to blood, and it just pushes up all my organs and bones out of the way, or maybe it's turned them into liquid too. I can't really tell anymore.

"I'm sure it's funny if you think about it a certain way," said Otis with his trademark smile. "So now, every day at 3 pm, Lloyd the Doorman calls the elevator car down to the service level where he gives me my bucket of food. It's pretty much all I do."

"What about going to the bathroom?" asked Teddy.

"Nope," answered Otis. "It all just turns to blood."

As sad as that was to hear, it gave Hellen an idea.

"I need to go talk to Lloyd the Doorman. Perhaps he's seen the little boy that I'm looking for," Teddy said.

"Ok, well be safe out there," Otis waved goodbye as the elevator doors closed on his face.

One day, Teddy thought with a smile, he's going to pop and it's going to make a giant mess.

CHAPTER
THREE

Lloyd the Doorman was quite tall and very pale and had a friendly enough demeanor. Demeanor seems like it should be a nasty thing, since the word sounds like *demon* and *mean* smooshed together, but it's actually used to describe the way you look and behave around other people. Ironically, while Lloyd the Doorman had a friendly enough demeanor, he actually did have a little bit of a mean demon side to him. If you got on his nerves, he could get very impatient and had a way of manipulating you.

When someone manipulates you, and listen up children, because this is important, it's because they think you are foolish and easy to control. People who do this are often very sad and lonely people. But are also very smart. Or at least smart enough to learn how to fool you.

Lloyd asked, "What's good about it?" as he stood by the door, the freezing air whipping his neck and legs every time he opened and closed it, as the girls ran up to greet him with a "Good Morning, Lloyd!"

Lloyd had always wanted to be an inside worker, allowed to mingle with the guests of the hotel like that damn elevator asshole used to do. He would reminisce about how back when the hotel was in its prime, he would open the door to the most lavish and wonderfully dressed ladies and gentlemen going inside to get drinks at the bar and dance in the ballroom. But he never got to see any of it. Just standing there all night, ushering people in and out of a party he was never invited to. A lament he was happy to share with Hellen and Teddy.

"Why don't you ask our father to promote you? He's the boss of the hotel, right?" Teddy asked the doorman as she climbed the stone wall around the entrance of the hotel, tip-toeing from stone to stone like a ballerina-spy.

Hellen looked out into the driveway of the hotel. It was quite beautiful in the winter, sitting atop a long steep road, almost as if it were on the crest of a mountain. Teddy liked to pretend that she was a giant, living above the clouds waiting to eat up any trespassers who would dare climb the beanstalk and invade her home. Hellen looked out at the snow and thought of how lonely this hotel ultimately must feel, which is why it probably keeps all the ghosts and never lets them

SIMON ORÉ MOLINA

leave. She thought about how the cold made people act badly, sometimes.

"Delbert isn't the boss, Teddy, he's just the caretaker. Or was." Hellen said into the cold air.

When you speak outside and it's cold, your air will sometimes hang in front of your face like a puff of smoke. Your words suspended in front of you in a tiny word cloud.

Of course, nowadays, Hellen is a ghost and has no breath, and can't do this anymore. But Hellen used to love doing this when she was alive. Hellen wondered if she had an empty jar and caught the air inside it, back when she could breathe, if the words would be trapped inside it too.

Lloyd bent down and told Teddy that Hellen was right, their father wasn't the boss.

"Your daddy was just looking after the place for the winter. No one has seen the true Manager of the hotel in many years. Some of the other ghosts say the Manager still lives somewhere in the hotel," Lloyd wondered aloud. "Maybe you two should try and find him."

"That sounds like something you should do, since you're the one who wants a promotion. We have our own mystery to solve," Hellen said with a nod of her head.

"Oh really? And what mystery is that?" Lloyd asked, signaling to Teddy to be careful as she climbed the ivy-covered walls by the front door.

"There's a small, cute boy somewhere in the hotel.

Have you seen someone like that?" Teddy asked Lloyd.

"I never said he was cute," Hellen blushed.

"You basically said you wanted to marry him," Teddy laughed back.

Before Hellen could give her sister a much-deserved punch in the arm, Lloyd looked at Hellen and gave her a serious look.

"You saw a little boy?"

"Yes," said Hellen. "Teddy thinks I'm making it up but it's true. He was playing in one of the rooms. I hid behind a corner when I saw him, but when I peeked my head around to see, he was gone. But his little toy car was still there. I also saw him through the impossible window in the office and this morning I saw him running into the hedge maze."

"Do you still have the toy car?" Lloyd asked.

"Of course not. I didn't take it. That would be stealing."

"That would be stealing," Teddy said, trying to time it so she spoke it at the same time as Hellen.

"Teddy, what are you doing?"

"I'm trying to sync up our speech," Teddy said to her sister.

"Why on earth would you do that?" Hellen asked.

"I think it's funny," Teddy laughed before running back inside the hotel.

"So, you haven't seen a little boy around here?" Hellen asked Lloyd one more time, "I'm sorry little

Grady girl, but the only children I know of in the hotel are you and your twin sister."

"We're not twins!" Hellen protested.

"Yes, right," Lloyd said, "but if you did see someone new, it's probably nothing. But it might be something. And in case this nothing turns out to be something, I suggest that you go ask Sally. After all, She has the skeleton key to the hotel and cleans up every room at The Overlook. If anyone knows where a little boy might be hiding, it would be Sally."

"That's a great idea Lloyd, thank you!" Hellen said as she ran back inside the hotel to find her sister.

Lloyd stood in the sharp winds outside the hotel, and thought about the conversation he just had.

When you have been in a particular job long enough, children, you might one day find that even though you are good at that job, or at the very least not terribly bad at it, the job still makes you feel miserable and unsatisfied with your life. And that is the opposite of what a job should make you feel.

If life was fair, and children, I'm sorry to say there will be more times when it is not than when it is, but if life were more fair than it *usually* is, Lloyd would be doing something that gave him a sense of purpose and allowed him to be a part of the party.

The doorman thought his life would be better if he could change his job, but he'd been doing this job since before he was a ghost and had no idea what else he *could* do.

Lloyd thought about what it was he might *want* to do, and although he couldn't really think of anything specific, he considered what Teddy and Hellen had said, and mused that maybe he *should* try to find the Manager of The Overlook and ask for that promotion.

CHAPTER
FOUR

"Why are we in the parlor room?" Teddy asked, "We should go visit with Darla and Roger, they always have fun stories."

Darla and Roger were guests of the hotel who had died there many years ago.

"We're in the parlor," Hellen told her sister. "Because I need to find Sally. So she can help us find Santiago."

"But why are we looking in the parlor if Sally isn't here?" Asked Teddy in an exhausted way.

"Because" Hellen replied, "I don't know where to find Sally, but this is where I first saw the boy."

"The boy that no one else can see and that you're in love with." Said Teddy.

"Shut up you dumb shit." Said Hellen, but Teddy, knowing her sister all too well, said it at the same time.

"Ugh, don't mimic me, Teddy!" Both Hellen and Teddy shouted.

Teddy doubled over, giggling.

Hellen just shook her head and went over to the middle of the room to look around. Although Teddy wasn't wrong, *why is it that no one else has seen him?*

She imagined herself with the little blond boy she'd decided to call Santiago. Laughing together, running down the halls and playing. His eyes bright green and kind.

Hellen saw herself and the boy holding hands as they ran down the stairs, and into the lobby. Running right through the living guests during the summer season, and playing hide and seek during the empty winter slump.

Hellen smiled and almost didn't notice that Teddy was about to fall off the back of the Victorian chair she was climbing.

"Be careful" Hellen said, and Teddy caught herself, jumping from one chair to the next.

Hellen went back to the matter at hand, which in this case meant, focusing on trying to find clues in the parlor.

There are many ways you can get a good vantage point when you are trying to find the answer to a riddle, or a clue in a mystery. Sometimes the best strategy is to take a step or two back, look at the whole picture and that can lead to clarity. But other times, it's best to get right in the middle of the densest point. To check the details in case you missed something obvious.

Teddy was humming to herself as she balanced on one leg, it was the tune of the Elephant song, you know the one, where the elephants come out to play on spider webs and have enormous fun? It was a song that their parents would sing to them when they were younger and alive.

Hellen told her to please be quiet as she was trying concentrate on finding a clue. But when Teddy stopped humming, that's when Hellen heard it, and it stopped her cold.

She couldn't tell where the sound was coming from, but it was the same tune Teddy was humming seconds ago, only it wasn't a hum, it was a sharp, high-pitched whistle.

Teddy heard it too and smiled.

"It's daddy!" said Teddy.

Hellen remembered the night her father stumbled into their bedroom and chased them down the hallway and chopped her and Teddy up into little pieces. *CHOP CHOP CHOP!*

She remembered the smell on his clothing, cheap whiskey and wood chips.

She remembered the look in his eyes, vacant but resolved, almost kind. She remembered that her daddy was calm when he chopped them up, like he was chopping wood out back for the furnace.

He was always good at chopping logs.

He would sometimes stand outside in the cold air, chopping log after log and joke that he must have been a lumberjack in a previous life. Normally, after the end of his shift, Delbert would come into his daughter's room and give them each a kiss goodnight. But this time he barged in, whistling the little tune from the elephant song, and told them in a very calm voice that he would give them a ten-second head start. Five seconds for each daughter. Teddy, who was still mostly asleep didn't see the big shiny axe in their daddy's hand, but Hellen sure did.

There are moments in life when what are called *instincts* kick in. What that means, children, is that even if you've never been in a certain situation before, like for example being chased by a lioness in the jungle or having to pilot a plane as it nosedives into the ocean, and suddenly find yourself in that very situation, well then a part of your brain that simply does not want to die takes over and keeps you from going into a complete panic.

So even though the sight of Delbert Grady standing at the foot of their beds with an axe was, by all accounts, something that rightfully could and should have frozen

SIMON ORÉ MOLINA

Hellen to her bed in terror, Hellen's *instincts* took over and, grabbing Teddy by the hand, forced Hellen to run out of the room as fast as she could drag her little sister.

"Where are we going?" Hellen remembers a sleepy Teddy saying to her, annoyed that she was yanked from bed.

"Shut up. We have to be quiet."

"Why? What the hell is wrong with you?" Teddy tried to pull away and go back to bed, but Hellen held on tightly to her little sister's hand.

"We have to hide."

"From who, Daddy?" said Teddy, looking back over her shoulder. "That's the dumbest thing I ever heard. I'm going back to bed you idiot."

"Teddy, don't call me an idiot. It isn't nice at all! Besides if anyone is an idiot, it's you!"

Now children, you know it's never polite or proper to call someone an idiot, even if they are being one, but it's especially never okay to call someone you love names like that. However, when you're very close to someone, when you know them very well and you both know beyond a doubt that you love each other, then it's okay to call them these things, because they know you don't mean it and are just saying it in the moment.

"Just trust me you idiot, and follow me," Hellen said as she dragged Teddy by the arm.

Hellen remembered how she tried to hide in one of

the other rooms, but all the doors were locked.

"We have to go upstairs," Hellen told Teddy, still struggling to pull away from Hellen's grip, barely awake.

"Stop it, Teddy!" Hellen yelled.

"Why are we running away from daddy?" she mumbled sleepily.

"Because that's not Dad, okay. That's a monster and it only looks like dad to trick us."

"A monster?"

"Yes. And it's trying to hurt us, Teddy. It's trying to hurt us bad, so we have to hide. We have to hide, and we have to be quick and quiet about it."

"But why would a monster want to hurt us? Maybe we should ask it what it wants."

The sound of their father's whistling got closer, as Hellen pulled Teddy along towards another hallway. She heard footsteps closing in on them. The loud determined gait of their father.

"We can't, Teddy. We just have to run. And no matter what happens, even if that monster catches up to us, we're going to be okay because we're going to be together."

Hellen remembered running down the hallway. Normally it's fun to run down the hallway of a hotel when you are the only little girls who live there, racing from one end of the floor to the other, but this time it wasn't fun at all.

It's funny, isn't it? How the exact same activity can be both the best thing and the worst thing, depending on why you are doing it.

Hellen and Teddy ran down the hallway, but the echoes were bouncing around the walls so there was no real way of knowing if they were running away from their father's whistling or towards it.

Hellen gripped Teddy's hand tight and turned a corner where they bumped into a smiling Delbert Grady.

There are times in life when very horrible things happen, and there is no justice, no explanation as to why, and no last-minute escape.

Sometimes, children, life is just sad and unfair, and this is an unpleasant but important truth.

Sometimes it's easy to think that the only thing that is real is that the world is a horrible place.

CHAPTER
FIVE

B ack in the parlor, the sound of whistling faded but was still audible. The echoes in the hotel were strange and there was no way of telling when what you heard was right behind you or on the other side of the hotel or even on another floor. Their mother called it '*acoustics*', which is the way a room, or in this case a hotel, is built so that sounds can bounce around the walls like a super ball. The whistling got softer and softer until it disappeared.

Hellen realized that she had been clenching her hands into little fists. When she opened her hands up, she noticed that there were little imprints of her fingernails in her palms from where she was digging into her own skin.

Teddy was climbing on one of the ornate yellow

chairs in the room, balancing herself on one of the armrests.

"Why do you hate daddy?" Teddy asked, almost too casually, as she jumped from one chair to another, as if she were playing a game of 'The Floor is made of Lava.'

"Please be careful, Teddy."

"Be careful of what?" Teddy giggled. "We're already ghosts."

"You can still mess up the furniture and Mr. Braddock won't like that."

"Oh, dumb old Mr. B can lick my butt," Teddy jumped onto a coffee table, making the floor shake a little.

"I don't hate Delbert. I just don't like him much either."

"That's another thing, why do you call him that and not Daddy?"

Hellen didn't answer her sister. She was distracted by something she saw on the floor, by the bottom of one of the long, ornate yellow curtains in the room.

"What's this?" Hellen said to herself, but Teddy leaped off the table and ran over to it so she could see it first.

"It's a little toy car!" Teddy shouted before Hellen snatched it out of her hand.

"It must belong to the little boy!" Hellen exclaimed. "See, that proves he was here!"

"No, it doesn't." Teddy said, adding "But it's a good clue." So as not to crush her sister's silly game. Teddy didn't think that there was a little boy in the hotel, she just thought her sister was lonely and wanted a friend to play with that was her own age. One of the reasons Teddy liked it when people thought they were twins instead of just sisters, was that it made Teddy feel closer to Hellen, and assumed Hellen would like her better if they were the same age.

Hellen was staring at the little toy car and noticed a spot on the hood. It was deep brownish red and looked like dried ketchup. As she scratched it off the toy, she realized it wasn't ketchup, it was blood.

Drip drip drip.

Hellen heard it first, then Teddy. The sound of thick water dripping onto a wet spot on a carpet.

Drip drip drip, plop plop plop.

That's when Hellen and Teddy both saw it. The dark puddle that was very slowly spreading on the carpeted floor right below a fold in the yellow curtain. Right where they found the little toy car.

Teddy was back on the table, looking at the little dark red drips splash into the spongy carpet with a wet thwack-plop. Hellen walked to the curtain, *drip drip drip*, slowly grabbed at it, *plop plop plop*, and pulled it open.

When Hellen pulled the curtain back, she and Teddy saw the body of a young woman whose legs were badly broken and whose dark bruised neck was suspended by a course line of old rope.

One of her eyes was veiny and purple, and her lips were puffed and cut up. A stream of blood rolled down her thighs, off her ankles and into the small puddle on the floor.

"Hello Miss Carla," Hellen and Teddy said in unison.

"Why hello to the lovely Grady Twins!"

"We're not twins!" Hellen corrected.

"And what are we up to this fine winter's day?" Miss Carla asked.

"We're looking for Hellen's boyfriend that doesn't exist," Teddy teased.

"He does exist. And he's not my boyfriend! And yes, we're looking for him. See, this is his toy." Hellen held up the car for Miss Carla to see, "We found it near your blood puddle, you must have seen him."

"Oh, yes, the things I have heard and seen since my last night on this cruel world have been many! Have I ever told you, dear children, how it is that a young Miss Carla met her end?" Oh boy, thought Hellen, here we go. Teddy and Hellen had heard the story many times, but it never stopped Miss Carla from telling it to them again and again.

"It was many years ago, mind you," Miss Carla

started saying. "Many years before that father of yours showed up with you two and your mother in tow. Back when The Overlook still meant something in this community. Back when only the highest of society would be allowed on the grounds. Back then, I was really a sight to behold. But to really understand the scene, to really get the world right, I have to go even further back, to the night I first met the man who…"

"Uh, Miss Carla," Hellen interrupted, "we don't have time for this. We are in the middle of an investigation. We just need to ask you a question."

Miss Carla looked up, as if she had just been stung by a bee, and then nodded, "Very well, then. What is it you want to know?"

"Did you see who was playing with this toy car?" Hellen waved the little car in front of the woman's lopsided and swollen face.

"No, I did not!" Hellen's face dropped a little when she heard this. She was sure this was a clue, that this was proof that the boy was real.

"I can't see anything until someone removes this cursed curtain from my view. But I did *hear* someone in here earlier. I could hear them driving around in the room."

"What do you mean driving around? Like on a motorbike?" Teddy asked, she was back to climbing the furniture.

"No, you simple child, not like a motorbike. Like me. In my chair."

"Your chair?" Asked Hellen.

"You see! That's what happens when you cut off my tragic tale of despair and betrayal. You would not be asking so many stupid questions if you had just been patient."

"Do you mean your wheelchair?" Hellen asked.

Although Hellen had heard Miss Carla tell her story more than once, she never thought to retain much of the information because she knew that if she ever needed any details, she couldn't remember she could just go and ask Miss Carla.

"Yes, my dear. I meant my chair. That cursed chair that led to my most foul of ends."

When you hear a story you don't particularly like, it's easy to forget the details, but the truth is your brain, even if you don't like the story, will always store some of the information away, just in case it ever becomes useful.

"Yes, I remember now," Hellen told Miss Carla. "You were on your honeymoon, and you fell down the stone stairs outside. It splintered your spine into tiny slivers of bone, and they got into your bloodstream, into your lungs."

"You're taking all the drama and romance out of it, but yes, that's basically what happened," said Miss Carla.

"Then you spent the rest of your honeymoon in a

wheelchair. *Driving* around the hotel."

"That's when my husband ran off. Leaving me alone in this decaying palace to watch my youth rot away like the drying petals of a wilting petunia."

"You're weird," Teddy said casually from across the room. She was jumping from the back of a chair to the top of a loveseat. Clapping in the air when she jumped like some kind of excited, yet dim-witted, squirrel.

Hellen sometimes wondered how they could be related.

"Teddy, be nice. We need Miss Carla's help, and we shouldn't be rude."

"But she talks funny. Look, watch what happens when I ask her something. Miss Carla, why do you talk in that dumb funny way?"

"I speak with the eloquence of a once great debutante. It is you little urchins that use the common speak of the help."

"See?" Teddy said, giving Hellen a *told ya* look while she went back to climbing and jumping, trying in vain to reach one of the light fixtures that hung from the ceiling.

"Sorry about that," Hellen apologized to Miss Carla. "You said that you heard someone driving around in here. What did you mean?"

"I mean," said Miss Carla, "what I said. And what I said, as you may recall before your twit of a twin of a sister interrupted me, was that I indeed heard someone driving around the carpet."

"You could *hear* someone driving on the carpet, how is that even possible? Hellen, this wackadoo lady is full of shitbirds, let's go back to looking for Sally. I'm bored!"

"Teddy!" Hellen was hardly stern with her sister, after all, even though little sisters can be annoying and rude sometimes, you still love them and want to protect them. It's the job of the bigger sister to make sure the little sister is safe, but that also means that it's the job of the older sister to make sure the younger sister behaves and doesn't get both of you into trouble, or worse yet, in this case, make someone mad at you whose help you still needed.

"I'm so sorry Miss Carla, please don't mind her. She's been in a strange mood all day."

"Yes, I myself had a sister, not a twin mind you, but I know what a pain siblings can be."

"We're not twins," said Hellen.

"That's the spirit." Miss Carla replied, half listening to Hellen. Many adults often only listen to themselves talk, especially when they are speaking to children. It is a very rude thing to do, but it's a thing many are fond of doing, even if they are not self-aware enough to notice they do it. So, if you ever want people to care about what you say, make sure it somehow involves them directly, pretend to be into what they are into, and pretend they are interesting even when they are not. Lie if you have to, children, it's okay. If it means people will like you, it's fine to do practically anything."

Teddy still wasn't convinced and asked, "Are you sure Miss Carla, are you sure you heard someone in here?"

"Of course I'm sure, child. What an absurd question to ask an adult. That sound is etched in my brain for all eternity. Yes, it was a soft sound, but my ears have always been something to be proud of. Something to envy. I have always had beautiful ears that were also very good at hearing. The sound from earlier today in this very room, it reminded me of when I would be driven in my chair around the hotel. It was so lonely for a while, my husband left me, you know, couldn't be bothered to take care of his crippled wife, but there was a bellboy that would take care of me, drive my little chair wherever I chose to go. And that sound of the wheels on the carpet, that soft sound, was deafening to me. It was all I would hear every day. Did I ever tell you about how I paid that bellboy to kill me?"

"Yes, Miss Carla." Teddy and Hellen said together.

"Well, it's quite a story, children. And I will tell it to you. You see, when I realized I had lost everything, my legs, my spine, my husband, well I paid that young bellboy that would push me around, to put me out of my misery. I gave him 20 dollars, which wasn't that much then, but more than it is now, and told him I would expect him in my room that very night and gave the young man a copy of my key. I was expecting to be shot, or smothered with a pillow, you know, something dignified and befitting a woman of my stature, but instead the bellboy used the key to my room to come in and drag me by the hair, down the stairs and into one of the parlor rooms where the boy proceeded to do unspeakable things I dare not say in front of young children, to me. When the boy was done, he began to choke me with a thick tweed rope. It itched so much! I remember thinking of how much it itched and burned against my throat. He then hung me, the bastard fool, behind the curtain, which is probably the most insulting part about it. Couldn't even leave me to die in my suite. Now look at me, all bruised and battered and stuck in this uncomfortable position for all of time."

"About the boy though?" Hellen asks.

"Yes, yes. Well, I can't tell you if it was a boy or not, just that I heard someone going up and down on the carpet with a three-wheeled wheelchair."

"Three wheels?"

"Oh yes, a three-wheeled chair. Of that, I am absolutely certain."

CHAPTER
SIX

Hellen and Teddy were back in their room on the tippy top floor of The Overlook Hotel. Hellen was holding the little toy car they found downstairs and was looking under her bed and took out a shoebox.

She wanted to show Teddy a picture of Santiago, or whatever the boy's name might be, so that Teddy could see what she was talking about. But the drawings she'd already made of him didn't really show his face.

Hellen opened her shoebox, it was a really long one, the kind that might contain boots or clown shoes, the kind of shoebox that would have made a great coffin for an iguana, tail and all.

From the shoebox, Hellen pulled out her scrapbook. It was a thick scrapbook, although its pages were still mostly empty, with a cover made of white leather, bound with two stands of gold string that had been tied along the binding in bows. It had been a gift from her mother when they were alive. It was so Hellen could collect all her memories of her childhood in one place. Now she mostly used it for her drawings.

"Here's one of the boy playing with his toy cars on the carpet that looks like a snake. And this one is the boy running through the hedge maze, but you can't see his face in this one either," Hellen said, as she looked through her shoebox of drawings.

"These are really good, Hell," Teddy said. "You should be an artist when you grow up."

"We're never gonna grow up Teddy. We're ghosts."

"Oh, yeah," Teddy said. "Still."

"I'm just gonna have to draw a new picture of him so you can see his face better." Hellen looked in her shoebox but couldn't find her box of crayons.

"Have you seen my crayons?" Teddy said this at the same time that her sister asked it. "Oh my God Teddy, you're the worst!" They both said again.

"It's too easy." Squealed Teddy with delight. "I always know what you're gonna say."

"Well, I can't draw you a picture of this boy if I can't find my crayons."

"I'm sure you have been daydreaming about kissing his face all day. I'm not surprised if you lost your crayons while thinking of him," Teddy teased her sister.

Hellen decided to ignore this but still shot Teddy an angry look as she moved the old shoebox out of the way, looking for her crayons under the bed.

When she did this, she noticed something small was written on the wall, by the foot of the bed, something that was hidden from sight by the shoebox. It was written in red crayon, and all it said was OLLEH.

"Teddy, look at this! Did you ever notice this before?" Hellen asked, as Teddy came and crouched down beside her to get a better look.

"Olleh? What does Olleh mean?" Hellen asked.

"It's Hello backwards, duh!" Teddy said. "You can see it in the mirror."

Hellen turned around and saw what Teddy was talking about. She was right, it did say hello. "That's a neat trick!" Hellen said.

"It could have been the boy."

Hellen was studying the words written in red crayon on the wall.

"Yeah, or it could have been Mommy. You know she's not the same with that bullet in her head. Always doing strange bullet-head stuff."

Teddy grabbed Pugsley, her favorite spider, from his web and placed him on her face, letting him crawl around.

"Teddy, please stop that."

Teddy took Pugsley off her face and placed him on

her shoulder and walked over to her sister.

"Hmm, maybe you're right. It doesn't look like mommy writing. Does this mean the boy was in our room?"

As Teddy said this, Hellen looked around a little self-conscious. She pictured the little blond boy looking around the room and judging her, making assumptions about her life. She was mortified at the thought that he might think that the spider collection was hers and not Teddy's. He'll never want to be friends with a girl that has a spider collection! Why did her little sister have to be so strange? If the boy had indeed been in their room, she hoped the boy had the decency not to snoop while he was there.

While Hellen had her anxious daydream, she didn't notice that Teddy had ascended the dresser and was hanging her feet down by Hellen's head.

"Hellen?"

"Yes, Teddy?"

"How come we don't look like the other ghosts?"

Hellen looked up at her sister.

"What do you mean?"

"Well," Teddy said. "You know, how come we don't have scars up and down our bodies, or why aren't we in little bloody chunks? You know, Miss Carla is still hanging from that rope, and Mr. Braddock has that stab wound in his stomach, and even mommy has that bullet hole in her face. So why do we just look like we did before?"

Hellen looked at her sister, wondering why this was coming up now. Why wonder this now?

"Do you think," Teddy added, "it's because when we died, we were still little and when you're little you don't get punished as bad for getting yourself killed?"

Teddy had always been the strong one of the two, even though she was the younger sister, but in this moment, she looked very small and almost lost. Hellen rarely felt like the older sibling when she was with Teddy, but right now she looked at her little sister and couldn't help seeing her as this tiny baby she had to protect, only she wasn't sure if she knew how.

"I don't know, Teddy. Just help me look for my crayons okay? We have to find this boy before bedtime, or mom's gonna freak."

"Okay," said Teddy smiling. Teddy didn't let anything sit with her long enough to really upset her, Hellen thought about that as she looked at her sister playing with her pet spider and laughing; that must be really nice, Hellen thought.

CHAPTER
SEVEN

Teddy looked out the window of their room and down onto the gardens behind the hotel. The sun was clouded by the winter sky and looked like a murky marble in a bowl of milk.

Hellen peeked out the window and looked below them, to the patch of manicured lawn outside the hotel and to the left of the hedge maze trying to see if she could spot Sally the chambermaid in the courtyard, but instead she saw something else.

"Come, Teddy. Forget the crayons for now. Let's go ask Darla and Roger if they've seen anything."

"Finally," Teddy sighed, as she put a tiny leash made out of dental floss around Pugsley the spider's little body. "Something fun. Let's go Pugsley"

She patted the little spider's head, and followed Hellen out the door.

The Overlook gardens are quite lovely, even in the winter. Although the roses and honeysuckle were all in deep hibernation under the eight feet of snow that piled up on the lawns, the evergreen hedge maze and the topiary animals that guarded it, were still a sight to behold.

And that was why, regardless of how cold it got outside, you could always count on Darla to be taking Roger for a walk around the hedge maze every morning.

Hellen and Teddy rushed outside into the bright sunshine that reflected a blinding sheen on the fresh fallen snow. Holding their little hands over their eyes to shield the sun from their faces, the little girls ran over to Darla who had a tight grip on Roger's leash as he jumped around and dug his big paws into the snow.

Darla was a tall woman, a wiry frame covered in a large winter coat with a fuzzy collar, long pink winter gloves that went passed her elbows. Her hair was cut short, with midnight black bangs hanging just below her eyebrows, and a streak of white down the left side. She looked like a younger Cruella de Vil, one that wasn't yet as hardened or evil.

"Good morning, Darla. Good morning, Roger," said the sisters in unison. Hellen shot Teddy a glare, but

Teddy was too busy petting Roger on the head to notice.

"Good morning my darlings." Said Darla, and ashed her long thin cigarette in their direction. She was holding a purple and black parasol, shielding her from the sunshine.

"Good morning girls," said Roger through the slit in his dog mask.

Roger wasn't actually a dog, just a grown-up man dressed in a full-body dog suit with a strange plastic mask that made him look like a fuzzy cartoon dog and not so much a real dog.

Roger did this because it was his sexual fetish. A lot of grownups have these, children, because they get easily bored with things and want to live a life where nothing is boring. Some grownups like to get tied up, like they were being held against their will, as part of a game. Some like to pretend they are other people and put on wigs and costumes and speak in accents that aren't their own. Some people like to rub themselves on mannequin legs in fancy stockings. Roger, for example, thinks that dressing up and acting like a dog, and sometimes a bear (depending on his mood) and being forced by Darla to perform sexual acts for other guests of the hotel, is the best way for him to feel good about himself and make his life less boring.

It was also, according to Roger, the best way for Darla to prove she loved him. I know, children, that this doesn't make much sense, but grownups rarely do.

"Would you two darlings please come help me with Roger? He's being an absolute nightmare this morning."

Roger looked up at Darla with a sheepish smile.

"Am I going to be punished?"

"Be quiet Roger, *people* are talking." Darla smacked Roger in the spot on his mask where the snout was, with the handle of her parasol.

Roger whimpered and crawled away, but it was very clear he loved it by the way he wagged his tail.

Now when you are about to ask something important of a grownup it is good form to be polite. But also to be clear with what you want to know. The sisters had just learned from Miss Carla that grownups tend to meander when they give answers. Having been misinformed, that the more they talk the smarter they may appear to be. When mostly all children know that smart people keep it short and sweet.

"Miss Darla, we need to ask you something important," Hellen said, as she walked up to the woman with the parasol. "It's about a little boy I've been seeing in the hotel."

"A little boy, you say? Oh, my darling little darling, you must be imagining things. The hotel is closed for the winter, so there are no guests. And I personally know every specter here, and there are no children in the hotel, I'm afraid."

"Other than us," Teddy said from behind Darla.

"Yes, of course. Other than you darlings, how silly of me."

"But I saw him," Hellen insisted. "It was a little blond boy, he was wearing a red sweater. Miss Carla in the parlor says she heard him in there, riding around on a three-wheeled wheelchair. And we found one of his toys."

Hellen took out the little car and showed it to Darla. Roger came over to sniff at the toy, but Hellen instinctively pulled it away to protect it.

"No Roger. This is not a chew toy. This belongs to the little boy in the hotel."

"Hellen is in love with him," Teddy laughed. Pugsley was crawling in and out of her mouth as Teddy did.

"Shut up Teddy," Hellen glared at her sister. "I'm not in love with him. I don't even know him. I just am curious as to why there is suddenly a little boy in the hotel. It would be nice to have a new friend." Hellen told Darla, "Someone my own age."

"What about your twin sister?" growled Roger.

"We're not twins!" Shouted Hellen with Teddy mirroring her, saying it at the same time and undercutting her point.

"You sound like twins to me," Roger smiled and went back to digging around in the snow with his big doggy paws.

Darla took the little toy car from Hellen, and just like that, the toy began to fade away, as if slowly being erased into a mist.

"What did you do!?" Hellen screamed.

"My darling child, I did nothing at all to your little vehicle. It simply vanished in my hands when I grabbed a hold of it to get a better look. But I do believe that I know what that is now. Or was. Or rather wasn't."

"What do you mean?" Asked Hellen

"Do you mind if I ride Roger?" Asked Teddy

"Of course you may not ride Roger, he is not a plaything." Darla batted Teddy away.

"At least not for children." Added Roger with a growl, nipping at Darla's ankles, hoping for another swat to the snout. But Darla merely kicked at him.

"As for you child," she said to Hellen. "There are things about this old hotel that are not for young fragile hearts like yours to understand. This hotel has a strong energy my darlings, it's what binds us all here. It's what keeps these things that keep happening here, happening."

She put her cigarette out into the snow. Smoking is such a nasty habit, children and one should never take it up, but if you are going to be around someone who smokes, it's cool to not be a dick about it and just let them enjoy their wonderful right to do it.

"You see, my little hazelnuts, back when I would throw the most lavish parties The Overlook had seen in the better part of a decade, that's ten years darling."

Hellen knew what a decade was, but she didn't dare

stop Darla from talking. Darla hated being corrected even more than she hated being interrupted.

"And in that time, and all the time since that time, mind you darlings it has been quite some time and then some, I have seen a lot of ghastly and terrible things."

"Like what!?" Teddy asked, a little too excitedly. "Pugsley wants to know."

"Oh, things I daren't say to children. You know, people being buried alive, guests being drowned or hanged, the odd tongue ripped out of some poor chambermaid or bellboy's mouth. Ripped out, mind you, not cut off, but ripped with brute force! Grown men cut up like jack-o-lanterns by their wives, guts and blood strewn about like old stockings. Wives bashed-up like crumpled newspaper by their husbands, their caved-in faces unrecognizable. Ghastly rapes and murders and parties where people had too much fun, things of that nature, children. Not at all suitable for young ears like yours."

"But you said you knew why the little boy's toy disappeared just now."

"I did?" Darla said, while lighting a fresh cigarette.

"Yes dear, you said you knew what it is, or was or rather wasn't. Something like that." Roger growled.

He was squatting over a patch of ice, pretending to shit.

"Oh yes, I guess I did. It's just that you shouldn't trust everything you see in this hotel. The hotel has a way about it, almost as if it had a heart and a brain. Like certain rooms in The Overlook have a dark, dark soul.Sharp teeth that the hotel uses to eat up energy. And you should just be happy it hasn't gobbled you right up, yum yum yum. And the same goes for your little twin over there with that spider in her mouth."

Hellen looked over at Teddy and Pugsley, who quickly scuttled out of Teddy's mouth and sat quietly on the top of her head, as if caught misbehaving when he should have been paying attention.

"So you see," Darla continued. "Sometimes the hotel has been known to anticipate something special or the hotel might have a daydream or be reliving a memory. But what you're seeing isn't real. It's a projection but it isn't real. Like a ghost."

"But *we're* ghosts," Teddy said.

"Yes, but we're *real* ghosts. I'm talking about the ghosts in your head that no one else can see. *Fake* ghosts."

"But not everyone can see *us*, and we're real. What's the difference? Why can't there just be ghosts for ghosts?" Hellen asked Darla.

"There *are* ghosts for ghosts, they just aren't real ghosts. You see? Most ghosts often are ignored, they are looked over, so we begin to get so lonely we manifest the things we want. We invent a thing that isn't there to make us feel better about how we feel. The hotel does that too. It can be having a daydream and you might be seeing it, but it's not a real ghost. Does that make sense darling?"

It didn't. Hellen was learning an important lesson at a very young age, and children, you can learn it too, most adults have little to no idea what the fuck they are talking about and it's okay to call them on their bullshit.

But Hellen didn't call Darla on her bullshit. She also didn't just take her word that the boy must just be a fake ghost. She knew he was in the hotel somewhere. She just had to find him.

CHAPTER
EIGHT

The one good thing that came from having talked to Darla and Roger was what Darla had said about the hotel being alive. That it had memories. Maybe that's what Hellen was seeing.

"You think you're seeing a memory of the hotel?" Teddy asked Hellen as they walked down the first-floor hallway. "What's that Pugsley? You're right, Hellen is losing her shits!"

"Teddy, you don't even know what you're saying."

"It's Pugsley who doesn't know. I'm just repeating what he said!"

"All I know is that if it's a memory, maybe I can find out more about him. Maybe he died here a long time ago and we just have to find his ghost. Or maybe," Hellen said to Teddy, "It's a memory that hasn't happened yet."

"You're becoming obsessed. It's not healthy."

Hellen ignored Teddy and kept explaining her theory.

"Time doesn't have to work in a straight line, Teddy. Or even a circle. Time can be a mess of wires all crossed together."

"Like a spiderweb?"

"Yes, Teddy, exactly like a spiderweb. Time crisscrosses through itself and so sometimes people remember things before they happen. Maybe that's what's going on here."

"It makes more sense that it's an old memory if it's a memory at all," Teddy said. "That's what Pugsley thinks at least. He also thinks we should have some lunch and you should stop being a crazy stalker and leave this poor kid alone."

"Tell Pugsley to mind his manners and remember I can crush him between my fingers. I know which web is his."

As if on cue Pugsley hopped off Teddy's shoulder, climbed her head and hid underneath the little blue hair clip in Teddy's hair.

Hellen loved to read, and so it made sense that her favorite room in The Overlook was the library.

Teddy, who loved to make up stories as she went along didn't much like reading, thought the library was very boring. But she did like to climb the ladder and ride it around the circular shelves, which was very distracting for Hellen.

When they got to the library, Hellen grabbed a pile of books about the history of The Overlook and some books about the dead, to try and find out something, *anything,* about ghosts that can only be seen by other ghosts. Something to clear up the mystery of this phantom little boy. But she kept coming up empty.

"It's not in any of these books about apparitions or specters or phantoms!" Hellen said, "It's not in any of the necromancer or necronomicon or necrophile books! There's no spell or recipe or receipt, not a rhyme or reason or rhetoric I haven't looked up and I can't find a thing! Just piles of old maps and newspaper articles cut out from something called *The Rocky Mountain News.*"

Hellen took out a stack of loose papers that were tucked away in the corner of a bookshelf. She flipped through them, skimming over them to see what they were. "These seem to be papers about Horace Derwent?"

"Who's Horse Dermot?" Teddy asked from atop the ladder, climbing onto the bookshelf.

"Horace Derwent," Hellen corrected, "was the owner of the hotel. *This* hotel. Look at this stuff, there's all these articles about him, old contracts, even an ad from the *New York Times.* Look," Hellen held up the full-page ad from the travel section.

There was a picture of Derwent, he was bald and wore rimless glasses over a nose that sat on a pencil-thin mustache that made him look less like a millionaire mogul and more like a snake oil salesman.

But there was something about his eyes, like they were looking at Hellen from the picture, that made her fold the papers up and put them into the large front pocket in her dress. For some reason, she thought they were interesting enough to keep. maybe put into her scrapbook. They were interesting, but unfortunately, of no real use to them.

"Look at this Teddy, it's a really fancy invitation to a Masquerade Ball. Look at the date, August 29, 1945. That's when the hotel opened. Do you think this is the ball that Darla is always talking about?"

"Darla is pretty cool," Teddy said, half listening to her sister.

Hellen put the fancy invitation in her pocket with the other papers and looked up as Teddy kept talking.

"How she talked about the house being psychic and stuff. I wonder where the house's crystal ball is." Teddy thought out loud, "I mean, if the house is psychic then it should have a crystal ball."

"Darla didn't say the house was psychic, dummy. She said it was conscious. That it had a brain and a heart."

"Well, the heart's the furnace, everyone knows that," Teddy said.

Hellen nodded in agreement. The furnace and boiler in the basement of The Overlook filled the entire room and were by far the biggest and oldest the girls had ever seen. A giant ancient thing, which thumped and hummed and pumped out heat and life to the hotel, lying in the core of the place, like a large napping tiger. A rat-king of ducts and pipes functioned as the hotel's circulatory system and zigzagged upward into the high, cobweb metropolis that was the basement ceiling.

"Of course the furnace is the heart," Hellen agreed "so where could the brain be?"

Hellen got an idea; she remembered an old blueprint that Mr. Braddock had been looking over one day when he wasn't just organizing keys on hooks. It had been the original blueprints of The Overlook. He had wanted to get them framed and place them behind the front desk, but he never got around to it. Too many keys to organize, she supposed.

Hellen dug around a big box of old papers and maps, rummaging through them as if they were a chest of old blankets. Teddy and Pugsley had a view from the top of the library and from where they sat it looked like Hellen was being eaten by a big pile of hungry maps.

"Aha!" Hellen cried in triumph. "I found it!"

Hellen unfolded a large piece of paper that took up most of the floor of the library. She had to push tables and chairs out of the way in order to get the blueprint fully open.

"I can't see anything from here. I'm too close," said Hellen.

She looked up at Teddy.

"Can you see anything from up there?"

"What should I be looking for?" Teddy asked

"I don't know, look for something out of place, a room or a part of the hotel you don't recognize."

Teddy looked down and saw the layout of The Overlook. It was very big. From the service quarters, to the kitchen, the Colorado Lounge, the laundry rooms and all the guest rooms and suites, there was the impossible window, the one that looked out onto an outside that wasn't there. There was the walk-in freezer, near Cook's small sleeping quarters. She could see the whole hotel laid out, from the boiler-filled basement all the way to their room on the tippy top floor, the place seemed endless - and it didn't make any sense. Doorways were put in places that lead nowhere, hallways led to dead ends that circled back into themselves in ways that were constantly impossible and contradicting.

It seemed to Hellen and Teddy that the Hotel actively and joyously participated in confusing its guests. It was another reason the girls liked living there.

Teddy was proud to see that she and her sister had practically explored every inch of this massive place at one point of another. But what was that? There seemed to be another room above their room.

"There's a room above our room," Teddy said.

"What do you mean there's a room above our room? Our room is on the tippy top floor. Mom always says that."

"I know. But look, if you take three steps to the left and four steps to the up and then one step to slightly down, you'll be standing where I'm looking and you'll see that you'll be looking at it too."

Hellen followed her sister's directions and ended up standing right where their room would be in the blueprint. And sure enough, there was another room right above theirs labeled *attic*.

"It's an attic. I'd say that's a good place for The Overlook's brain."

Hellen smiled as she looked at the map.

Teddy slid down the ladder with poor little Pugsley hanging on for dear life. She ran over to where Hellen was standing, to get a closer look.

"I think this is important, Teddy," Hellen said. "I've been in almost every room in the hotel when we go exploring. We've been all over the hedge maze and the playground and the staff rooms and this was never on any of the hotel maps on the walls. There must be a reason why the hotel keeps this hidden."

"Yes," said Teddy. "Pugsley says the attic must be fucked."

Hellen shot her sister a stern look but let it slide.

79

"Wait a minute, that's a great idea Pugsley!" Teddy jumped up and down almost flinging the little spider right off her head.

"What now?" Hellen asked.

"Pugsley says we don't have to go to the attic, because my spiders can go everywhere. They can help! We can go tell them what you saw, and they can help us search the hotel. It will be much safer than going to the attic ourselves and Mom never has to find out that way we can still go find Sally and ask her is she's seen Santiago and we'll be in back in our rooms before bedtime!"

Hellen considered this, although she wasn't crazy about the idea of having to get close to Teddy's spiders, she had to admit it was a solid plan.

"Okay, Teddy, let's use the spiders."

"Let's go tell the others, Pugsley," Teddy said to the little friend on her shoulder, "they're going to be so excited."

CHAPTER
NINE

Teddy had ten pet spiders and there was something about each of them that made them unique and special. Before she set them off to help Hellen with her hunt for a ghost that probably wasn't a real ghost but that still could be a hotel memory-ghost, she wanted to make sure that Hellen knew each and every one.

"This is Rose, she's the Alpha Female of the group. She's a southern black widow but she is very friendly and affectionate. She's the oldest of the spiders. I consider her my co-parent." Teddy pointed to each spider as she spoke about them, letting them crawl in and out of her hand as she pet them with her tiny thumb.

Hellen had never gotten this close to the spiders before, and this was because Hellen thought spiders were scary gross. But she also knew that they weren't really dangerous. They, like Hellen herself, just wanted to be left alone.

"This little guy is Ghostpepper," Teddy went on. "He's a regular house spider but is standoffish with other spiders. Kind of like he's better than them. Huh Ghostpepper, you think you're better than other spiders? But he's not though," Teddy assured Hellen.

"Over here you have Bacon. Bacon is kind of the badass of the group. She's a Bold Jumper and has awesome adorable eyes, see?! She also spins curse words into her web. It's hard to make out but, okay see, this one says 'piss balls' on it!" Teddy nuzzled Bacon who nuzzled her right back.

"Bacon is tough and likes to jump on things like me! But she's also as soft as a kitten. Do you know there's really no difference between a house cat and a jungle cat except its size?"

"Yeah of course I do. I told you that."

"Oh yeah, sorry. Do you want to hold Bacon?"

"I'm okay thank you. You can just keep telling me about them if that makes you happy."

"Okay!" Teddy smiled and she rushed over to the closet and picked up Mary.

"Mary is a Goliath Birdeater. She's a big, beautiful tarantula. Look at her golden hair and happy face! She might be the biggest, but don't let that fool you. She is very quiet and shy. Much shyer than Snow, who's the smallest. See? That's Snow - the one with the soft white hairs growing out of her knees and eyes. I think she might have a superpower because she can wiggle those hairs around and catch things with them even though the hairs growing out of her eyes make her blind."

"That doesn't seem normal or healthy, Teddy."

"Yeah, Snow's the best!" Snow's little white hairs tingled in the air and oozed a sticky green gel, she then retreated to her web in Teddy's closet.

"Maïa is the guardian of the pack, she's a Marbled Orbweaver and she is quick to protect any of her siblings. She's like the Hellen of the family." Teddy said, and her sister couldn't help but smile.

It is a very nice thing when you find out just how much someone who loves you loves you, and in the case of Teddy comparing Hellen to one of her spiders, which was the highest honor Teddy could give and Hellen was very honored indeed.

"Mellick is a Zebra Spider, see his cool stripes? He is very neat and tidy for a spider, always cleaning his web. He's also the only vegetarian spider I have, and he always releases the bugs he catches in his web. Instead of bugs, Mellick eats candy, and beer gummies are his favorite. I guess he takes after me." Teddy said, giggling.

"Buckle is the crabbiest spider there ever was. I think he might secretly be a crab pretending to be a spider so he can live here." Teddy shook her head like a loving but frustrated parent at Buckle. "Get it together dude." She told him as she watched him try to rebuild his web.

"He might not end up being very useful today," Teddy admitted to Hellen.

"Then we have Kingsley, The Diving Bell spider. Kingsley seems scary but is actually very sweet. He loves the females of his tribe and makes sure they always eat first and have strong webs. He doesn't really care about the males in the group. He's cool but he's also a bit of a dick because why not let the ladies do their own thing? They know what they're doing mister. We don't need your help! I love him though. The sweet dummy," Teddy smiled and looked at Hellen

"And of course Pugsley, total mamma's boy," She said patting Pugsley with her pinky finger.

"So that's the gang. I'm sure they'll help us find your memory boy."

Teddy took Rose from her web and brought her up to Hellen's eye level, because when you are speaking to any member of any species, it's always polite to do so at eye level.

"Go ahead," Teddy said, "tell her what you need them to do."

Hellen walked up to Rose the spider and whispered something into her little spider ear and watched as Rose went scurrying away.

"She's going to go investigate the attic while we split up and search the rest of the hotel," Hellen told Teddy.

Teddy was happily impressed with how Hellen took to spider talking.

"Great, you should take one of them with you," Teddy said. "Who do you want?"

Hellen smiled, "Why not Maïa? After all, the Hellens of the group should stick together."

"Awesome!" Teddy handed Maïa to a hesitant Hellen.

"So do I just, what do I do?"

"Just put her on your shoulder. She's cool. And don't ignore her if she gives you advice. She knows what's up. If anyone can help solve this mystery, it's my spiders!"

And with that, Teddy was off and running with poor little Pugsley hanging on for dear life.

"Where are you going?" Hellen called after her. But it was too late, Teddy was already out the door and down the hallway before Hellen had a chance to blink.

"Well Maïa, any ideas on where we should start?" Hellen asked the spider, but it was more a question for herself.

She looked out the window and saw that Teddy was already outside by the hedge maze. Typical, Hellen thought, she just wanted to split up so she could go play outside. *I don't think that's what she's doing. You should give your sister the benefit of the doubt.*

What was that? Hellen heard thoughts ring out in her own head, but they didn't come from her.

Of course they didn't come from you, they came from me.

There it was again. It was like there was a tiny little voice inside her head thinking out loud, but quiet.

It's me, Maïa. Said the voice. *Remember, I'm on your shoulder. Don't freak out. If you freak out too hard, I could fall, and you could accidentally step on me.*

"Oh my god. Maïa! I didn't realize you could talk!"

Well, you've never let any of us this close to your ears before.

Hellen realized this was true and she felt bad about it.

Don't feel bad. I never made an effort on my end to get to know you better either. We're both at fault.

"Can you hear my thoughts? Why can you respond to the things I'm thinking?"

I don't know. I'm just a spider. All I know is I can hear you.

That's amazing, thought Hellen.

Yeah, it's pretty cool said Maïa. *Want to go explore this bitch? Try to find that cute little blond boy?*

Hellen smiled. She knew she couldn't hide what she was thinking from Maïa, so she just smiled.

Why do you like him so much? I can tell you've been thinking about him a lot, but I mean you don't even know him.

'I'm not sure why,' Hellen thought, and the little

spider spied on her thoughts. 'I guess it's because I just thought I would be alone forever. I mean I know I have Teddy and Mom and everything, but I thought I wouldn't ever be able to grow up, to play with other kids. I mean I know I will never get older, I'll never get married, or have my own kids but I don't know, it's dumb.'

No, it isn't.

'I mean, it's dumb for me to think that just because there might be another kid stuck in the hotel that it would change anything. I mean, he might not even like me.'

But then again, he might. Like you, I mean.

'Yeah.'

Listen Hellen, I'm just a spider, so I may not be the best source of advice for you in this moment, since what I think is important is very different from what you think is important. But I will tell you this, you have to find this little boy because you'll clearly be haunted by him either way.

"Okay Maïa, where should we start?" Hellen asked the little spider on her shoulder.

Let's start with room 117. I have a feeling about it. Said the spider.

CHAPTER
TEN

"Your feelings are hardly ever right, you silly pissface," Teddy said with a laugh that echoed in the wind. Pugsley wanted to go outside to the hedge maze so now Teddy was standing in the harsh winds. Pugsley told Teddy that this time was different. That he had a *feeling* about this feeling. Teddy rolled her eyes. "It's getting late and the sun will be going down soon, Pugsley. We'll have to be back in our rooms, you know how mommy gets when we're not in our room at bedtime." Teddy's voice got softer when she said the next part, "Mommy can be just as scary as anything else in this place." Pugsley nuzzled up to Teddy's neck and rubbed her cheek with one of his fuzzy little legs, as if to comfort her.

Teddy looked out at the entrance to the snow-covered hedge maze. There was a ladder by the entrance of the maze, probably used to help the gardener trim it, Teddy thought to herself. Even though the whole place was covered in fresh snow, Pugsley noticed that the ladder didn't have any snow on it at all. *That's strange*, thought Pugsley and hopped off Teddy's shoulder to get a closer look. "I'm bored, let's just go back inside!" Teddy yelled at the spider, but Pugsley was already sprinting across the snow, insisting they explore the hedge maze a little more. Teddy shivered as she made her way towards Pugsley who was perched on a small hill of snow at the entrance to the maze.

"I'm serious Pugsley! I'm going to scoop you up and put you in my pocket. This is ridiculous, I want to go back inside!"

And that's when Teddy saw him. The boy. Hellen's boy! I mean it must have been him. It *must*. Who else could it have been? She only caught a glimpse of him as he ran into the hedge maze, wading through the snow in a hurried panic, barely visible out of the corner of Teddy's eye, but it was clearly a little blond boy that just sprinted by.

She didn't believe it! Hellen was telling the truth. She sure felt like a rotten little sister for not believing her and she made herself a promise to make it up to her big sister by ghost busting this little boy.

Teddy smiled wildly and tucked Pugsley safely under the bow in her hair.

"Hang on Pugsley, we're going to go catch us up a ghost boy," She smiled and pet Pugsley's tiny little head with her pinky finger.

The spider nuzzled her finger and dug his eight little legs into her hair to hold on. When she knew her little friend was safely buckled in, she took off sprinting into the maze. She was so focused on running as fast as she could that she didn't notice the topiary animals turn to see her enter, and that some of them had slowly started to follow her in.

Back inside The Overlook, Hellen and Maïa were walking down the first-floor hallway towards room 117. "What's so special about this room?" Hellen asked the little spider.

I'm not sure. Call it Spider intuition.

"Why can't I just call it intuition? Why does it have to be all spidered up?"

Because Spider Intuition is so much better than the regular kind.

"This room is right below our mom's room," Hellen said, ignoring the spider's comments.

What do you mean?

"I mean my mom is in this same room. But just

one floor above us. Why did you pick this room Maïa?"

I didn't pick this room, little one, I just felt it calling to us. Now, let's see what we find inside.

Hellen walked up to the door, little Maïa perched on her shoulder.

"The doors are usually locked. There's no way we'll get inside."

Give it a try little one. Maybe we'll get lucky.

There was something about the way Maïa was talking that was strange to Hellen, as if Maïa already knew what was about to happen but was pretending she didn't. It was a strange way of speaking and Hellen was suspicious, until she reminded herself that this was the first time she had spoken to Maïa and maybe this was just how the spider always spoke.

Hellen reached for the doorknob to room 117, but before she could grab a hold of it, the door swung open, as if softly pulled open from inside the room. When Hellen peeked her head in, she saw that the room was empty. Oh, there was a bed and a mirror, other furniture to be sure, but no other people or ghosts.

"Hello?" Hellen asked the empty room.

It's empty. Said the spider on her shoulder.

"Yes, I can see that," Hellen huffed. "But sometimes it's better to say hello just in case."

Oh dear me, I believe we might have hit a dead end.

"Wait, what's that?" Hellen noticed something on

the floor at the foot of the bed and walked inside the room. "It's my box of crayons!" Hellen exclaimed as she picked it up off the floor. "But a lot of the crayons are missing. How on earth did they end up here?" she asked.

SLAM!

Hellen and Maïa looked up to see that the door, which was wide open a moment ago, had slammed closed. Startled, Hellen rushed over to the door, but it was locked. She pulled and pulled at it, but it wouldn't budge. Being a ghost in a haunted hotel meant that you were usually the one doing the scary things that made the living guests uneasy, but even ghosts can be spooked, children. Because in the end ghosts are just another version of people, and people, deep down, will always be frightened of things they don't understand. It's fear that helps keep us alive, even when we are dead.

Maïa ran down Hellen's shoulder and down her arm until she was standing on Hellen's finger.

Hold me up to the lock. Let me see if I can fix this.

Maïa jumped off Hellen's finger and disappeared into the keyhole.

Hellen looked around the room, not liking the feeling of being alone. Even when you are the kind of child, like Hellen, who enjoyed playing by herself or would rather read a book than talk to someone she didn't like, feeling lonely is a terrible feeling and quite a different one from being alone. When you are alone you are spending time with yourself, which can be a very fine and rewarding thing to do, but when you are lonely, you are spending time without anyone, and you realize how empty being stuck with just you can be.

Hellen felt very lonely the moment Maïa disappeared into the keyhole. And when Hellen felt lonely or anxious, she buried her head in the corner of a room. Pressing her nose right up against where the walls touched.

So that's what she did. She walked to the nearest corner and buried her face into the wall. Which is precisely the moment when she started to see them.

At first, they were blurry, hidden in the shadows of the room, but up close Hellen saw tiny frantic words written in red crayon, scribbled all over the wallpaper.

And more seemed to be appearing, like waxy blood stains, across the walls of the room.

Outside, Teddy was running after the little boy inside the maze. It was hard to keep up with him, because it looked like he was trying to get lost on purpose. Teddy called out to him, but he didn't slow down. He seemed terrified.

"I'm not gonna hurt you! My sister likes you! Hold up!"

But it was no use, the boy just ran faster and deeper

into the maze. At one point the boy doubled back and walked over his own footprints, and Teddy almost caught up to him, but when he turned a corner and Teddy followed, he was gone. Like he disappeared into a dead end in the maze, swallowed up by the twigs and ivy.

Teddy looked up and realized she didn't know where she was. She wasn't paying attention when she was chasing the boy and now she had no idea where to go.

But this wasn't a problem for Teddy because Teddy loved to climb, and this was a perfect opportunity for her to work her skills!

She dug her feet into the hedge, finding a sturdy enough branch inside the bushy green wall, and made sure it could take her weight. She lifted herself up to the top, carefully balancing on top of the hedge, and if you've ever climbed on top of a hedge before, well you know that it feels a little like you might imagine what walking on the top of a cartoon cloud would feel like. Sturdy enough to hold you, but one false step and you'd fall right through! But Teddy's been a climber all her life, and this wasn't the first time she'd been on top of a hedge.

She looked around, trying to get a better idea of where she was in relation to the exit. From above the maze, she couldn't really see the hotel, but she could see she was not far from the center of the maze, and she knew she could easily find her way out from there.

But before she could climb back down and head to the center, she noticed something a little off. Teddy could see that some of the hedge animals weren't where they usually were.

Normally the animals are outside of the maze, surrounding the entrance like soldiers, but Teddy noticed one of them was actually in the maze, hovering above the wall. It was a lion with a large green mane, and it was only a few hedge walls away from her. The lion's claws, made up of thick pointy branches, were extended towards Teddy.

She stared at the lion, which was frozen in an odd position, like she just caught it trying to move but it froze the moment she looked at it.

"What a stupid place to put the lion. I wonder why they moved him here."

Before Teddy could get a better look, she heard something behind her. Like the sound of snow being shaken off a large dog that had been covered by a blizzard.

She turned in the direction of the sound and saw another large topiary animal, one she'd never seen before. It was also inside the maze but in the opposite direction of the lion, right behind where Teddy was standing precariously on the top of the hedge wall.

It was longer, much longer than the other animals she'd seen, and appeared to have a big grass triangle growing out of its back. A row of sharp thorns lined its big open mouth.

"It's a shark!" Teddy squealed. "Hellen! You have to come see! I found a hedge shark!"

Near the shark was a fresh pile of snow. That's why she hadn't seen the shark before, it had been hiding.

Teddy was so excited she didn't notice that the lion, which she wasn't looking at, began to creep closer to her, its long claws growing sharper as it prepared to pounce.

"Hellen!" Teddy yelled out for her sister again. "You're missing it!"

CHAPTER
ELEVEN

Hellen was still locked inside room 117 of The Overlook Hotel. She was looking at the scribbled words on the walls. There were notes written all over with tiny colorful words, just like the backwards 'Hello' she had seen in her room.

She began to read:

Em Truh Yddad. Edit Ynnad Edih, Ynnad Edih, em pleh. pohc pohc pohc pohc pohc.

Only not all the words were written backwards. Some were upside down.

pɐpp⅄ Hnɹʇ Wǝ Hǝld Wǝ pɐpp⅄ qǝpp⅄ ɥnɹʇ ɯǝ ɥǝ ɥnɹʇ ɯǝ ɔʎod ɔʎod ɔʎod.

And some were upside down and backwards!

¡sɹnɥ ǝɯ sɹnɥ ǝɥ pɐq pɐp ⅄uuɐp dlǝy.

Some were what appeared to be just jumbled up

letters that meant nothing.

She tried to make out what some of them said but it was hard, the words were so small.

She could make out some of the phrases that had been written and crossed out, over and over, but they didn't make any sense: *dremur mruder* and *duddy hamster*.

The words seemed to be multiplying in front of Hellen, spreading all over the walls and even the ceiling. The sound of crayon nubs being scratched against the wall getting louder and louder. It sounded like a windstorm. The waxy red crumbs of crayon staining every inch of the room.

Hellen just watched as this was happening, unsure of what to do. Reading the words over and over and over in her head, trying to make sense of them. *Pohc pohc pohc pohc pohc!*

Outside in the hedge maze, Teddy was staring at the topiary shark and wondering why her sister wasn't answering her. When Teddy turned back towards the hotel, she noticed the leafy lion that was three walls away was now two walls away. It's as if he had jumped to the next wall, getting closer to Teddy. She noticed that the lion's claws were longer.

"I wonder if these dumb things are actually moving around," she asked Pugsley, who shrugged his eight little shoulders.

"I mean this is a very haunted hotel. Just because I've never seen them move around doesn't mean they don't."

She looked at the holes in the hedge animal that functioned as the lion's eyes, its expression seemed to have changed.

"I mean this lion is obviously moving."

She inched closer to get a better look, but Pugsley tapped her on the shoulder with one of his legs, motioning her to turn around.

"What is it Pugsley?" She looked over and saw the shark was now closer than it was before. Its large mouth open wide, showing more rows of thorn teeth.

"You're right," she said to her little spider "It's like a game of red light green light. They only move when you don't look at them!"

She turned to the lion, and sure enough, the lion had inched a little closer to her.

Teddy stood there, balanced on the top of the hedge, with a shrub shark on her left and a leafy lion on her right.

Sometimes it's important to listen to your instincts, children. These *instincts* are what help us survive and face our fears or, in cases of our fears being reasonable, like say being stuck between a shark and a lion, our instincts help us run away and avoid the threat all together. But sometimes, when we are brash and young and foolish, when we are perpetually bold and six years old, what we are left with is an impulsive little ghost who follows her gut and Teddy's gut told her to attack the shrub animals.

Unlike Hellen, Teddy didn't like to stop and think too much about anything, she liked to act. To be in the moment. And so without thinking too much about what would happen, she leaped onto a branch coming out of the top of the hedge wall closest to the Lion.

"Hello little lion. You wanna wrestle, is that it?"

But when she turned back to look at the hedge shark, who was now starring at Teddy with a clenched jaw, the lion took the opportunity to strike.

"Ow!"

Teddy looked back at the lion, frozen in place, and then looked down to see a long gash in her arm. A trickle of black smoke-like blood oozed out of Teddy's arm and hovered in the air.

She grabbed her arm in pain, incredibly shocked by what had happened, and jumped back to her center hedge, between the shark and the lion and keeping an eye on both.

She wasn't prepared to get hurt. She didn't think ghosts *could* get hurt. But there she was, with a deep cut in her arm that felt like electric wasps were tearing their way through her tendons.

Teddy was trying to calm her breathing. She held her arm tight against her side, to dull the pain. She thought about what Hellen would do in this situation. Hellen would be calm and calculated and try to have the problems fix themselves. She wouldn't be rushing into a fight with these things before thinking about a plan.

That's it! Teddy realized.

"Pugsley, I think I figured it out."

She smiled at the little spider as she turned away from the shark for just a moment and let it inch closer to her. She faced it and it stopped.

But now the lion started to make its way closer.

Teddy giggled to herself and nodded to Pugsley.

"It *is* Red Light Green Light!" Teddy said.

Red Light Green Light was one of the games Hellen loved to play most, before she became a ghost, she would make Teddy play it all the time.

Teddy took a look at where both the shark and the lion were in relation to her, she bent her knees and readied herself. She turned her back to the shark and faced the lion.

"Red light lion. Green light shark!" She yelled.

She stared at the lion, its mouth open, melting drops of snow made it look like the lion was drooling. Teddy turned around and yelled out.

"Red light shark. Green light lion!"

Teddy arched her eyebrows, making a funny face at the shark which was frozen about four feet away from her. The shark's tail was curved inward, like she interrupted him mid tail-stroke.

She laughed knowing that if she had a pair of garden scissors, she could cut the shark's tail off or stab the lion in the eye. She smiled at how easily she could be the one chasing them. She turned to the sky and saw the sun was getting close to setting. They should be getting back to their room, it would be bedtime soon.

Behind her she could feel the lion getting closer. She could hear its soft growling as it prepared to pounce.

"Red light lion. Green light shark!"

Teddy jumped and turned to face the lion as it froze in its tracks. The loin's claws just inches from Teddy's face.

She could hear the shark cutting through the air, swimming towards her and the hedge lion. She could feel it getting closer.

Teddy smiled, "Okay you dumb *fuckshits*, here we go!"

She closed her eyes and heard the lion roar as he came to life. The shark and the lion were right on top of her, but right at the moment when both predators were about to strike, Teddy relaxed her stance on the branch she was standing on and let herself fall through the flimsy roof of the hedge wall, disappearing into the thickets and leaves below as the shark and lion collided, digging their spiky thorny teeth and sharp branchy claws into each other above her.

"Teddy!" Teddy screamed triumphantly, pumping her little fists in the air.

Back inside room 117, Hellen was trying to read all the messages written on the walls, but the words kept piling up on top of each other, making it very hard to read them even if they weren't all jumbled or backwards or upside down, and Hellen was feeling overwhelmed. She remembered how in her room Teddy had used the mirror to see the word Hello, she ran to the vanity mirror and looked at the reflection of the walls in its shiny face.

It was still hard to make out, but she thought she could see the word *Danny* or *Daddy* written over and over. She could read the word *Help* or was it the word *Hurt*? Maybe it was *all* of those words. But she couldn't be sure.

This was not like the books she read in the library. These words were scribbled on the walls like a notebook of first draft ideas, like a yellow pad brainstorm. What Hellen's mother called 'Scratch Paper Thoughts'. The walls looked like someone practicing how to write a message over and over and over again. *dremur mruder duddy hamster.*

Hellen focused on the walls in the mirror. Trying to make out as much as she could before the words got scratched out or covered with different words. There was the word Danny again, yes, she could tell it said

Danny this time. And there was the word hurt, but it was upside down. She noticed that on the floor, by the wall, was the nub of one of her red crayons. She rushed over to it and picked it up.

"If Teddy were here," Hellen said to herself. "She'd say something like, 'Why don't you write on the walls and see if they answer.' Or something else equally absurd."

But Hellen didn't have any other ideas, all she could hear in her head was Teddy's voice telling her to just go ahead and write on the wall, even if it didn't work, it would be fun.

So, with little to lose Hellen grabbed the crayon and wrote, 'Hi.'

She looked at the word written on the wall and then at the wall itself. Nothing happened.

Then she realized something. She crossed out the word 'Hi' and wrote 'iH' instead.

And that's when the spot on the wall right below her 'iH' answered her, as red waxy letters appear on the wall: 'yeH.'

'?ouy era ohW.' Hellen wrote below that.

'.yrots ruoy ot tnatropmi ton m'I .ti tuoba yrrow t'noD'

"?sdrawkcab gnihtyreve ctirw ot evah uoy oD" Hellen wrote on the wall.

"No." Said the wall. Hellen sighed, it would have been hard for her to continue writing everything backwards.

'Are you the little boy I've been seeing around the hotel?' Hellen wrote on the wall.

"Not quite." The wall responded, "You mean Danny. I'm Tony. But he is the reason I'm practicing."

"Practicing?" Hellen's crayon was running out of wax. She was down to the smallest nub.

"Yes. It's complicated. I only get one word. And I am debating which word to use. How to use it, you know?"

Hellen didn't know, but she had to move to another part of the wall to find out, since there was hardly any wall space left that didn't already have crayon on it. She was able to write one more thing, and for some reason she decided to let Tony know her name.

"I'm Hellen," Hellen wrote with the very last bit of crayon.

"Well hello Hellen," Tony replied by writing on the wall, "I'll try to tell Danny you're looking for him."

"Danny! Is that the boy's name?" Hellen yelled this out, but the walls didn't answer. She didn't have any more crayon left, and when she turned to look for her box of crayons that were under the bed, they were gone. Frustrated Hellen kicked the wall and started to tear at the wallpaper.

"Answer me! Is Danny the little boy? Where is he?" But Hellen got no response. But then all of a sudden, the writing on the walls started up again. But it wasn't answering Hellen's question, it just kept writing more of those frantic backward words. Hellen looked into the mirror and noticed the words were bolder, larger and easier to read. There was the word *help* backwards but also the words *killer*, *dead* and *murder*, all backwards and written in large red letters. Hellen, now officially spooked out, ran back to the door. Still locked. Where was that useless spider and why hadn't she unlocked the door? "Maïa, where are you?" Hellen yelled into the keyhole. "Open the door. Please!" She looked back at the walls, the words were bigger now, huge red letters. *pleh yddad ynnad daed redrum rellik retsmah dremur.* The words kept pilling on top of each other, getting bigger and bigger. Hellen went to bang on the door one more time but before she could, the door popped open, and there, on the other side was Teddy, covered in leaves and a few scratches but otherwise fine, her arm already healing. Teddy smiled at Hellen, Pugsley and Maïa waved to Hellen from their perch on Teddy's shoulders.

"Teddy, thank goodness," Hellen said and rushed out of the room, slamming the door closed behind her.

"What the farts were you doing Hellen!?" Teddy asked, a huge smile on her face, "You missed the hedge shark!"

CHAPTER
TWELVE

"I'm sorry I didn't believe you Hellen," Teddy said, walking with her sister back towards the lobby.

"It's okay Teddy."

"Still best friends?" Teddy asked.

"Still best friends," Hellen said.

"So, I'm pretty sure the boy's name is Danny."

"I like Santiago better. What should we do now?" Teddy asked her big sister, letting her two spiders crawl in and out of her nose.

"What do *you* think we should do Teddy?"

Teddy beamed, her sister rarely asked for her advice, and she felt very touched that Hellen seemed to really care what Teddy had to say. Just because you're older doesn't mean you have all the answers, the grownups in the hotel sure proved that to Hellen today.

"Hmmm," thought Teddy, "if the hotel really does have a brain, maybe it has ears too. Maybe it can hear us if we ask it a question. And if it's psychic maybe it will know where the boy is going to pop up next."

"Darla never said it was psychic."

But Teddy was already standing on a chair in the hallway yelling out to the hotel.

"Mrs. or Mr. Overlook, this is Teddy and Hellen Grady asking you if you can help us solve the mystery of Danny the little blond boy."

They held their breaths, even Maïa and Pugsley were tight-lipped, waiting for the hotel to answer. But nothing happened. Again, Teddy called out, "Oh Great Overlook, can you please tell us where the little boy will show up next?"

Again, they waited for an answer. And again, no answers came.

"Ok," says Teddy, "maybe this is just a normal, old hotel with nothing special about it."

"Except for all the ghosts," says Hellen.

"Yeah," Teddy agreed, "except for all the ghosts."

The sun would be setting soon, and the girls knew they should be heading back to their room to wait for their mother to tuck them in. But they hadn't solved the mystery of the boy and weren't ready to call it a day just yet. After exploring the first four floors looking for clues, they walked down the main staircase to the lobby and that's when Hellen spotted Sally the chambermaid walking with her cleaning cart on the other side of the lobby.

"There's Sally! Wow, I had completely forgotten we were supposed to be looking for her! That seems like days ago. Teddy, I'll be right back, I have to go talk to Sally."

"But it's almost time for Mommy to come and check on us," said Teddy. "We need to be in bed soon!"

Teddy, usually the sister who would happily ignore the rules, knew better than to disobey a Mommy rule.

"I'll only be a moment." Hellen sprinted across the lobby towards Sally and her big cleaning cart that was always full of fresh warm towels and tiny bottles of hair soap and mouth shampoo and regular old body cleaner.

Normally, Hellen and Teddy would be bugging Sally for samples. Or for a ride up and down the hallway in her cart, which could move pretty quickly once you got rid of all the fresh warm towels and the tiny bottles of hair soap and mouth shampoo and regular old body cleaner. But not today, today Hellen just wanted answers.

"Sally! We've been looking for you all over!" Hellen said breathlessly as she sprinted up to the cart.

"Hello one of the Grady twins," said Sally.

"We're not—it doesn't matter. Listen," Hellen said.

"You clean every room in this hotel, right?"

"Sure do, except for that room with the crotchety writer in it, 213, they don't pay me enough to do that! Just kidding, I'm dead, they don't have to pay me a thing."

Sally was the kind of grownup who always tried too hard to be friends with children. You know the kind, girls and boys, the kind of grownup that thought talking in funny voices and saying dumb jokes will get you to like them instead of just feeling very sorry for them. Sally was one of those grownups.

It might have been because she never was able to have children of her own back before she was a ghost, or it might be because she just wanted everyone to like her so much she was oblivious to the fact that her whole demeanor was off putting and desperate. But the fact was she never felt comfortable with just being herself, so she put on this big show for people, hoping that they would feel entertained.

Sally leaned down and gave Hellen a smile and nodded to Teddy as the younger sister ran up and joined them. Sally told Hellen and Teddy that every room had a ghost and that she'd seen them all—but the more Hellen described Danny the more Sally nodded her head.

"Sure doesn't sound like any ghost old Sally has ever seen. Unless they were hiding under a bedsheet with little holes for eyes! Wouldn't that be something.

A ghost like they show in those old moving pictures!"

Sally laughed and smacked herself on her own knee. The girls stared at her in silence.

Teddy asked Sally about the hotel being psychic and Sally told them that was nonsense.

"That's nonsense," Sally said. "Or as the nuns would say, *Nun* of your business. But I'm just joking around kids. The hotel isn't alive, and it doesn't have a brain. It's just a deeply haunted hotel with a history of tragic deaths and murders. It's nothing out of the ordinary and nothing for you two cute little devils to be worried about. This is winter break, the time to go wild because there's no one at The Overlook but us g-g-g-ghosts."

Sally gave each of the girls a tiny bottle of conditioner.

"Now go play with this tiny bottle of conditioner and leave old Sally to do her dirty work."

But before Sally could push her cart towards the elevators on the other side of the lobby, Hellen stepped in front of her.

"Do you have the key to every room?" Asked Hellen.

"Of course I do little Hell, I got the skeleton key, and it opens all the locks at The Overlook. More like The Over*priced*, hahaha, just kidding kids! But don't worry, this skeleton key is not made of bones. Haha."

Sally did a little skeleton dance that did not land with her intended audience.

"What about the attic, do you have a key for that?"

Teddy asked, tired of Hellen tiptoeing around it.

Sally's face dropped, her smile turned into a terse and tight-lipped scowl, and she got real close to Hellen and Teddy's faces.

"You two little pieces of shit better stay the fuck away from the attic, you hear me! I mean it! That's no fucking joke. It's closed off. Off limits. Besides, the door's been hidden, covered up, and the Skeleton key doesn't work on it, so don't try any of your little fucking bullshit and try to steal my key, you little whores, because I will fucking end you, and even if you do, even if you manage to get your disgusting dead little fingers on my key, it won't work. Now you godawful bitches get the hell out of my way, and if you tell anyone we had this conversation, and I mean anyone, and I mean any part of this conversation, I will fucking end you. I will find a way to kill you little twats all over again! Do I make myself clear!?"

Hellen and Teddy just nodded at Sally with shocked looks of disbelief. It's never fun to be yelled at by a grownup. Even when you haven't been doing anything wrong, having a grownup yell at you can make even other grownups feel tiny and helpless. And that's how Hellen and Teddy felt at that moment.

"We're sorry," they said in unison. This time Teddy didn't mean it as a joke, it just happened naturally, but it still managed to annoy Hellen.

"That's fine, you are only children after all." Sally smiled, softening.

"You don't know any better. Now run along and play, and let's not ever talk about what we were just talking about that made me so mad. Okay?"

"Yes," said Hellen.

"Okay," answered Teddy.

"Now get going children, and stop putting your noses where they don't belong. Like a stinky butt or a smelly onion soup! Haha. Am I right girls?"

Sally walked off, pushing her cart towards the elevator.

Hellen watched her go and shook her head. Hellen was mad at Sally for calling them '*only* children'. Hellen thought it was a dumb thing for Sally to say. Hellen and Teddy believed that the attic was the hotel's brain, and they believed the door of the attic to be locked, so in order to get to the brain to ask the question about the boy, the two girls would need the key, and no 'No' from any adult was going to stop them.

Teddy watched as Sally walked by the concierge desk and towards the elevator where she struggled to push her cart inside a tiny compartment in which Otis took up eighty percent of the space.

The clock by the check in counter let Hellen and Teddy know that it was almost past their curfew.

"We're not going to be able to figure this out today," frowned Hellen. "It's almost bedtime and mom will for sure freak on us if we aren't in bed. She always says the dangerous ghosts come out at night."

Hellen knew the responsible thing to do was get her little sister and herself back upstairs to the tippy top floor, but she also knew that without the attic key, she'd be up all night staring at the roof thinking that beyond that locked attic door there might be the answer to the mystery of the little blond boy.

The attic door would be like a scab in her mind that wouldn't heal if left alone, the kind of scab she had to keep scratching, until it bled and hurt and exposed the rawness underneath.

Teddy saw all this when she looked at her sister. Saw it in the sadness behind her eyes. She knew that she couldn't let her sister give up, and that's when Teddy noticed the box of keys.

The box that Mr. Braddock filled up and emptied out each day!

The box with a copy of every key to every room in the whole Overlook Hotel!

Surely the key to the attic would be there somewhere. Teddy smiled and turned to Hellen to share her plan.

CHAPTER
THIRTEEN

Hellen and Teddy took the stairs to the second floor. They thought if they could get some rope and a magnet, they'd be able to steal the key from Mr. Braddock.

"Why are we going to visit Mr. Duke's room?" Teddy asked. "I'm asking for Pugsley. He wants to know."

The two spiders, still on Teddy's head, wiggled their legs in the air.

"Because he's a strange hoarder and he probably has a rope and a magnet we can borrow."

Before Teddy could ask her next question Hellen said, "Because we need a rope and magnet to steal the attic key from Mr. Braddock, remember?"

"Uh-huh," Teddy mumbled, but it wasn't at all convincing.

"Teddy, this was your plan!"

But Teddy was already running down the hall towards Mr. Duke's room, not listening to her sister at all.

Teddy ran up to room 213 and knocked as she opened the door and walked inside. Teddy always had the tendency to open a door as she knocked on it, never waiting to see if she had been granted permission to enter. She would have made a terrible vampire, it's a very good thing she was a ghost.

The room was piled high with crumpled papers and clouded in smoke that made it look like a dusty rain cloud had gotten stuck in the room and tethered itself to the mold in the carpet.

The shelves and tables in the room were cluttered with Mr. Duke's collection of oddities and specimens that the man had collected when he was alive. Jars full of severed hands, conjoined skeleton babies, and shrunken heads preserved in formaldehyde took up all available space in the room. A taxidermy bust of a two-headed calf hung above a small writing desk *on* which sat an exhausted Smith-Corona typewriter, and *at* which sat an annoyed Mr. Duke.

He was dressed in a long elegant black coat that

draped over his shoulders like a cape, an ornate onyx cane that he balanced on the floor with his left palm, wobbled back and forth. He was looking over a fresh page he had just finished typing, as Hellen and Teddy made their way through the piles of papers and stacks of spooky ephemera that created a mini maze of clutter, spanning from door to desk.

Mr. Duke was staring at the page, his lips moving furiously as he half read it half-aloud and half to himself. He sighed angrily and tore the paper from the typewriter, crumpling it up into a little ball, *which looked like a little paper boulder*, Hellen thought to herself as Mr. Duke tossed it into a giant pile of little paper boulders behind him.

"It's very rude to interrupt an artist when he's at work children. Unforgivably rude." Mr. Duke said, rubbing the sides of his head with his thumbs and not looking up at the girls.

He sighed again, deeper this time and looked at his Smith-Corona with anger, guilt and contempt. The kind of look you might give your mother when she yells at you for doing something wrong, like being late for bedtime, even though nothing happened and you are safe so she should just relax.

Mr. Duke turned away from his typewriter, not being able to look at it. It sat there on the table, taunting him. He turned to face Hellen and Teddy, partly annoyed at their presence but also happy for any excuse to stop working.

"However," Mr. Duke said. "Seeing as I haven't been able to write anything that's worth more than a dead dog's dick in decades, then maybe some healthy procrastination might be just the thing to get me back into the flow."

"Still working on that book, Mr. Duke?" asked Teddy, eyeing a skeleton in the corner, wondering if the bones would be sturdy enough for her to climb.

"What a dumb thing to ask," Mr. Duke replied, without hiding any of the contempt in his voice. "I don't know little girl, could it be, *you stupid child*, that I'm working on the same damn book I've been trying to finish for the better part of thirty years!? The same goddamn book that has been haunting me since I set foot in this cursed hotel!? That book!? Yes, goddamn it, I'm still working on that book!"

Mr. Duke got up from his desk and kicked at a stack of papers near his feet. They went flying in all directions as his leg kicked straight through the pile and his body flailed. His pale face tried to blush, but there was no blood in his body. The way he died had made him the palest ghost at The Overlook.

Mr. Duke sat back down at his desk, lit a cigar and placed it inside a long glass ashtray and let the smoke just waft up and fill the room. He placed a fresh piece of paper into the Smith-Corona and stared at it, childishly ignoring the two little girls who stood next to him.

"We actually came to see if you could help us," asked Hellen, trying to gloss over the fact that Teddy just upset Mr. Duke, and hoping that she could distract him by talking about anything other than his book.

Alas, children, I fear this is something you will have to come to terms with when dealing with grownups, they love to talk about themselves, even and sometimes especially, when what they talk about brings them pain or sadness or frustration. Grownups love talking about their sad lives and how everyone should feel sorry for them. Grownups are horrible people and it's a very lucky thing that Hellen and Teddy will never become them. In fact, children, never feel bad for any of your friends who die young, for they are spared the cruel joke of becoming an adult.

"Help you!?" asked Mr. Duke, "No one was here to help *me* with my book! No one was here to guide *me* or give *me* notes or keep *me* on track! But there is no apparent limit to the number of little girls who just barge into my room to ask for favors! There is no shortage of those!"

"We just need to borrow something for a mission, Mr. Duke," Teddy chimed in, trying to help Hellen.

But this just pushed Mr. Duke further, he stood up, towering over the girls.

"Well I need things too! You think it's easy to be a writer at The Overlook? It's very, very difficult! You have no idea what this hell has been! What this hotel does to anyone trying to create!! When I first got here, I would get hundreds of ideas in my head, dozens of incredible lines of dialogue and prose. It would make you weep! But something happened when I got here, some cruel trick," his voice got quiet as if he realized he was being too loud and didn't want The Overlook to overhear him. "This place, it feeds off bad things. It wants bad things to happen. Because it makes it stronger."

"What do you mean?" Hellen asked.

"I mean mind your own business or at least stay out of mine!"

Hellen knew Teddy had made things worse by bringing up Mr. Duke's book, at this rate they would never get the key. Hellen looked out the dirty window in Mr. Duke's room, it was caked in filth, but she could still make out the sunset. The colors somehow bleeding through the decades-thick layer of dead spiders and dust.

CHAPTER
FOURTEEN

M r. Duke had been working on his novel since before he was a ghost at The Overlook. In fact, that is the exact reason he came to the hotel in the first place. To write. Mr. Duke's dream had always been to be a writer, to write an epic and amazing story that could be shared with the world and cement his place in history.

He heard that The Overlook was secluded and enormous, the kind of place you could wander around for hours and rarely see another soul. A place where you could tap into an unending well of inspiration. And that's exactly what it was, children, at first.

At first, the hotel was wonderful, and in the first few days that he was there, Mr. Duke's head flooded with ideas! It was as if a faucet of creativity had opened, and perfect phrases, wonderful words, and truly incredible stories came pouring out of him.

But Mr. Duke found all too quickly that the gift was an evil trick, a prank that The Overlook was playing on him. For even though, while wandering the halls of the hotel, his mind would brim with ideas, when he would go back to his room and sit at his desk to write, nothing came. Not a single usable word. Not one interesting phrase.

Every page the same thing, over and over and over. The same sentence, over and over and over. It was maddening. It didn't make any sense! He would sit down to write, a fully fleshed-out idea in his head, and yet nothing would come.

Eventually, he started writing by hand. But that didn't help. He found himself unconsciously scribbling the same sentence he'd been typing. The sentence would change every once in a while, but the outcome never did. He'd be stuck on one dumb phrase, one isolated thought that had nothing to do with what his book was about.

He wondered if this happened to everyone who tried to do something artistic or constructive at the hotel, but he couldn't bring himself to stop writing long enough to ask anyone else at the hotel if they were experiencing the same horrible artistic block.

Eventually, the repetition became a compulsion. He stopped leaving his room. As though the thought of new ideas coming to him, as he wandered the halls, that he never would be able to write down or retain, was torture. And he resigned himself to writing the same sentences over and over and over again. And although he dreaded the routine of writing the same thing a million times, severe headaches would overtake him when he wouldn't sit down to get the words out. The words were like poison in his body.

It was about that time that Mr. Duke, an avid admirer of the world of the occult, decided to stop using usual ink and moved on to his own blood.

Slicing into his wrists, he filled up an old ink bottle and began to write. For the first time since his arrival at The Overlook, he found that he could write down something new, something original and different.

Mr. Duke found that using his blood as ink made him somehow immune to this curse that had overtaken him!

He didn't know why, but he wasn't going to waste such an opportunity asking questions. For all he knew this too could be taken from him at any moment.

Furiously dipping a long and sharpened fingernail into the blood, he scribbled wildly, taking advantage of this marvelous new revelation. Writing as much as he possibly could, his finger trying to catch up to what was pouring out of his head! The blood ink was slowly clotting in its glass jar, he would need more, fresh from his veins, to keep the flow going.

Quickly, Mr. Duke cut deep into his gut, blood spilling out into a waiting bucket. Mr. Duke continued to write, as much as he could as the blood and life oozed from his body. It was worth it, though, his book was finally coming out of him, and it was glorious! All the work and the research he had done into the occult was paying off! All the ideas he had gotten while exploring the hotel, poured out of him.

Thanks to the Do Not Disturb sign that hung outside of his bolted hotel room door, his pale and bloodless body wouldn't be found for days. By then, Duke's ghost became trapped in the room with his own body.

When you're a fresh new ghost you don't really understand what's going on, and you certainly haven't yet learned how to interact with the physical world yet.

So the ghost of Mr. Duke was forced to stand there and watch as the pool of blood that spread from his wounds slowly engulfed the new pages of his writing, coating them, top to toe, in dark clotting blood.

His ghost just stood there, unable to move those pages out of the way. Unable to do anything but digest the knowledge that he would never again bleed, and never again be able to write.

Mr. Duke was at his desk, rubbing his temples.

"I'm sorry children, it's just that this place, this horrible place, it does something to you. It makes you feel like it can give you what you want, and I mean exactly what you want, but then it flips that want against you, makes you regret ever wanting it. The whole place is a goddamned Monkey's Paw!"

"Monkeys don't have paws, dummy, they have hands and feet like people," Teddy corrected Mr. Duke, but he just kept on talking over her, like adults do.

"This hotel, this place is a trick. Don't trust it. Don't trust anything it tries to show you."

"Actually, funny you mention that," said Hellen, happy to use anything as a transition to get her and Teddy closer to getting the magnet and closer to getting out of that room. "We've been seeing things, too. The hotel has been showing us something that we don't think is really there and we need to borrow some string and a magnet in order to figure it out."

Mr. Duke looked down at them, his fine features silhouetted in the light of the sunset, "I wouldn't go looking for trouble in this place, little girls. In this place, trouble doesn't need finding, it comes to you when you're asleep and crawls into your bed with a knife in its mouth."

Despite saying all of this, Mr. Duke was making his way to a set of drawers near his bed, which was covered in piles of paper that had the same sentence written on them, over and over. He opened the top drawer of the bedside dresser and took out a small U-shaped magnet and a long string of twine, extending his arm to hand the items to Hellen, but stopped short.

"Now, I'm only giving you these things because I'd like you both to leave me alone, and I'm not invested enough in your story to care what happens to you."

He looked over the two Grady sisters and considered his next move.

"But still," he added, "whatever it is you think you want to know, trust me, you actually don't. And even if you do, even if you get to ask the hotel to grant you a wish, it won't be granted in the way you want it. Believe me."

"So, it's true that the hotel is alive?" Hellen asked excitedly, her interest undercut by the fact that Teddy had asked the same thing at the same time to mimic her sister.

"Well, no. Yes. Kind of. It's hard to explain," said Mr. Duke.

"Try," said Hellen.

"Well, I don't really know myself. I just know that you shouldn't trust it." He sat back at his typewriter and started hammering out the same words he'd been typing when they had walked in on him. It seemed like he was signaling to the girls that visiting hours were over.

"Thank you, Mr. Duke!" Hellen waved to him as she and Teddy thanked him at the same time and both

Mr. Duke and Hellen shot Teddy a look of profound annoyance.

Mr. Duke said nothing as he watched them carefully make their way through his clutter and out the door.

CHAPTER
FIFTEEN

It was very much past their curfew when they left Mr. Duke's room and made their way to the elevators. Their mother was certainly going to punish them, *or worse*, so they had to hurry.

Hellen did not want them to bump into a certain ghost dad she'd been avoiding for years.

Teddy told Hellen that they would be in just as much trouble if they were two minutes late or twenty and they might as well stick to the plan.

Hellen hesitated. They had a magnet, and a rope. They could go to the lobby and try to get that box of keys and rush back to their room in the elevator. The risk of bumping into something dangerous would be low.

Hellen looked at Teddy, who seemed more intent on solving this mystery now than Hellen did and it made the older of the Grady sisters smile. This was *their* adventure now, not just hers. And she would see it through.

Hellen and Teddy started walking towards the stairs to head down to the lobby, but Hellen was so lost in her thoughts that she didn't notice they were going the short way to the staircase.

Normally they would have walked the long way, which would have meant doubling back to where the elevator was. But this time, they just continued forward in order to finish the loop the second floor and get back to where they started.

But as they went down the hallways and towards the staircase to the lobby, Hellen realized that they were about to turn into the hallway that led to room 257 and, as if by instinct, she grabbed a hold of Teddy's hand and squeezed it tight.

"Let's go back the other way. I don't like this way," Hellen said.

"What are you talking about dumb-butt? The stairs are coming right up. Doubling back would take us twice as long!" Teddy complained and tried to get out of Hellen's grip so she could keep walking towards the hallway.

"Well, just hold hands for now. I can't have you always running ahead and getting lost on me when we have lots of work to do," Hellen squeezed tighter.

But that wasn't why she held on to her little sister's hand. The hallway that led to room 257 was the hallway where Hellen and Teddy were turned into ghosts by their daddy. The hallway where they got chopped up.

"I don't mind holding hands with you," said Teddy.

"I love you too, little sister," Hellen said. And Teddy said it too, at the same time.

"Teddy, stop that!" Both Hellen and Teddy yelled, and Teddy giggled but Hellen got deadly serious and held her breath.

When they turned the corner, Hellen braced herself. Sometimes when she walked down this hallway she could see it, this vivid projection of her and her sister lying there, in a big messy pool of sticky blood. It was not something Hellen liked to see, and even though she knew it was just in her mind, that somehow made it worse, because it wasn't something she could just run away from.

You see children, when we carry something dark around inside us, like a memory or a resentment, it haunts us. Even when we are ghosts. And normally when something is trying to do you harm the smart thing to do is get away from whatever that is, but we can't run away from something when it lives inside us.

When Hellen and Teddy turned the corner, the hallway was empty. There was no blood on the walls or on the floors and no chopped-up pieces of her or her sister. Hellen smiled and gripped Teddy's hand a little tighter. As if giving her sister a hug through their hands. Relief spread through Hellen's whole body.

But then they stopped.

Both of them.

Frozen in place they looked to each other as if to make sure what they were seeing was real. There he was. The little blond boy.

Danny, or whatever his name was, came speeding around the corner riding a big wheel and stopping at the mouth of the hallway, opposite from the girls.

It was really him.

He was just as Hellen had described him, blond and cute with a white sweatshirt and a red hoodie over it making it look like a superhero's cape. His face was innocent but stressed, his hair was a funny bowl cut with bangs hanging over his eyes like a little raised curtain. He just stared at the two sisters staring right back at him. His cute little mouth hung open in confusion and fear. Hellen could see in his eyes that he too was lonely, and that he too needed a friend. It was amazing to see him that close, to be that near to each other.

He was riding a tricycle, the *three-wheeled wheelchair.* Danny had come around the corner fast, but made a sudden stop when he saw the girls.

Hellen looked right at him. All three of them stood frozen in place.

"Can he see us?" whispered Teddy to Hellen.

Hellen nodded back, she wasn't sure. From the looks of the boy, it seemed like he was staring right at them, but also through them. Like he was looking at something else that was also in hallway that the girls couldn't see. *'He looks so scared and lonely.'* Hellen thought to herself. She felt bad for the boy. She just wanted him to know that he was safe here, that he was with friends.

As if reading her sister's mind, Teddy nodded at Hellen.

"Hello, Danny," both Hellen and Teddy said.

Danny just stared at them. Unmoving.

"Are you sure that's his name?" Teddy whispered to Hellen.

Hellen nodded. "I think so."

They looked over at Danny, who still looked terrified.

Hellen and Teddy tried to reassure him, "Come play with us. Forever and ever and ever."

The little boy covered his eyes with both his hands and backed his three-wheeled bike away from them and around the corner.

"Why do you have to say what I say at the same time as me!" Hellen shoved her sister and let go of her hand.

"I think it's funny," Teddy smiled.

"Well, it isn't! It's off putting and creepy is what it is. You've scared him off! And why did I have to say, 'forever and ever'? That must have sounded so intense! Who even says that?"

135

Hellen and Teddy ran to the end of the hall, chasing him, but when they turned the corner, they didn't see Danny anymore. However, they did see someone else at the end of the hallway.

Standing in the doorway of their mother's old room was balding gray hair sitting atop a tall, twisted wire of a man, holding a limestone in one hand and sharpening an axe with the other. Smiling with a cigarette lazily hanging from his mouth as he whistled *The Elephant Song* to himself.

And this stopped Hellen in her tracks.

"Is that Daddy?" Teddy asked.

The excitement in her voice snapped Hellen out of her daze. But before Hellen could stop her, off Teddy went, running towards him.

"Daddy!" Teddy squealed as she ran.

You must remember, children, that Teddy hadn't seen her daddy in a very long time, and unlike Hellen, she didn't remember what had really happened to them.

But Delbert Grady didn't look up when Teddy yelled out for him. He just stood there, coolly, like a cowboy sharpening an axe.

"Teddy come back here!" Hellen demanded, fear

choking the words in her throat.

But it was no use, Teddy was running right up to her father, ready to jump and wrap herself around his legs. And as she did this, Teddy went right through him. Like he was not even there. And she fell on the floor behind him with a thump.

Hellen just stood there like a deer watching a lioness that's calmly stalking her, hardly reacting to how Teddy just fell through him as if he were made of light.

Was this why their mother never wanted them out after sundown? Did this gruesome thing, whatever it was, happen every evening?

"Huh? What's going on?" Teddy asked, confused.

I don't think this is real, said Maïa the spider, who was still sitting on Teddy's shoulder.

Hellen caught up to Teddy and looked at Delbert. He looked right through her as if she wasn't there. She tried to reach out and touch his arm, but it was as if he were made of mist. Her hands touching nothing but air.

"Why can't daddy see us!?" Teddy kicked at the image of her father, her little shoe going right through him.

Teddy remembered what Darla had told them, about the little toy soldier, that the hotel is powerful and sometimes it has memories that other ghosts can see.

"Hey, maybe this is just one of those rando Hotel memories. You know, maybe this is just like an old home movie of Daddy." Teddy guessed out loud, trying to make sense of what she was seeing.

Hellen caught up to Teddy and realized she was right. But it wasn't just any old memory of any old night that they were seeing. Hellen would never forget the empty look on her father's face when he gave them their head start that night. It was the same face that this memory specter-version of her father was making now. The same calm happiness in his whistling of the elephant song.

Hellen stood frozen in the doorway and watched as the phantom Delbert, axe in hand, headed down the hallway, as he whistled.

"We have to go," Hellen grabbed at Teddy's arm.

"No! I want to see what Daddy does."

"Teddy, I'm serious, I'm your big sister and you have to do as I say."

"You're just my *older* sister, we're the same size. And you can't push me around!" Teddy shoved Hellen out of the way, and because Hellen was so small for her age this was very easy for Teddy to do.

Teddy ran after her father as he turned the corner and went down the same hallway where they had just encountered the little boy on his three-wheeled bike.

"Where are you going daddy?" Teddy laughed as she skipped behind him.

Hellen heard her sister from around the corner, but

didn't move, didn't try to stop her. Hellen knew it was overdue that Teddy found out about what happened to them all those years ago, but Hellen had never found the courage to tell her sister the truth. This way was the cowardly way, but it was also clean and clear. For the first time all day, Hellen stopped thinking about the little blond boy and just braced herself for what her sister was about to see.

"Look Hellen! Come watch! There are memory versions of you and me here too! Hello memory Teddy! *Haha,* Hellen come see yourself! Hellen!"

But Hellen didn't need to go see. She'd been reliving this night in her head every day since it happened.

Teddy was smiling as she watched the image of her dad start to laugh as he chased his daughters down the hall, pretend brandishing an axe at them. Teddy didn't remember this at all, and so she was extra curious as to what was going to happen next, her little mind raced with imagination. Was he racing them outside to chop down a Christmas tree, she wondered? Was he letting them use the handle of the axe as the peg leg for a snowman pirate? Would he use the blade to create a— and that's when Teddy saw her father's face, calm and almost smiling, as he swung the axe into the memory version of herself.

The sound got sucked from the hall and it seemed to Hellen like the world was underwater. From around the corner, Hellen heard the soft whooshing sound of their father as he swung the axe, *whoosh!*, she heard the clear sound of the axe as it fell on top of either Hellen or Teddy's memory-bodies. *Chop!* And of course, because it was so loud, she heard Teddy scream and scream and scream.

When it was over, and Hellen saw the memory of her dad reappear around the corner, with his suit covered in blood. She watched him walk right through her and disappear into dust, like the toy soldier did in Darla's hand.

Hellen walked around to where Teddy was standing in the hallway. She noticed that the spiders weren't on Teddy's shoulders anymore.

"Where are Maïa and Pugsley?" she asked.

"I told them to go back to the room," Teddy said.

"Are you okay?" Hellen asked this, but she knew it was a silly question to ask. Even though they weren't twins, they were still sisters. Hellen could still feel Teddy's sadness.

Teddy wiped at her nose and took a deep breath. Hellen was in awe of her little sister, of how brave she was being. Teddy looked at Hellen and gave her big sister a nod, letting he know that she was okay.

Hellen wanted to say a million things to her sister at this moment, but she couldn't think of how to say any of them. As if the need to say so many things at once created a traffic jam in her brain and no words could come out even though she had so many of them. Words like *'I'm sorry for lying, I'm sorry for not protecting you. I'm sad, but I'm also happy we can share this now, but I'm so mad that this happened, and I think we didn't deserve this, but sometimes, in dark times I do think I deserved it, but* you *didn't deserve this, but still I'm glad that we're together'* words that got stuck in her throat and couldn't come out.

So instead of trying to find a way to say any of that, Hellen just hugged her little sister. Hugged her real tight.

"Let's go steal this fucking key," Teddy said.

CHAPTER
SIXTEEN

Hellen thought about what they needed to do in order to execute their plan with success.

"First," she said, "we need to distract Mr. Braddock and make him look away while we use the magnet to pull the box of keys off the counter and into our hands, allowing us to sneak that box into the elevator but having to make sure Otis doesn't rat us out. Then we ride to the tippy top floor and sneak into our room, making sure mom doesn't see us, and then we sort through all the keys to find the one that fits the attic lock. Then we go into the attic and find the hotel's brain and ask it about Danny."

"Cool jeans, jellybeans," said Teddy, smiling at her big sister. "Let's fucking do it."

The girls walked up to the busy concierge, who was

counting all the keys as he usually did. The box never left his sight, it would be very hard to get it from him without his noticing. Now they weren't proud of this, but in order to distract the dutiful Mr. Braddock there were forced to lie. They told him that they had met with the owner of The Overlook, and that he was very upset with Mr. Braddock.

"Oh is that so?" said Mr. Braddock casually, as he counted up the keys.

"Yes, it's so," said Hellen. "He says that he's been hearing complaints from the guests about how this place has become boring, and it was your job to make sure it didn't."

"Oh, and I suppose he was a little blond boy who told you that I was to give you the keys to the pantry so you could eat all the pudding you wanted. Nice try little twins."

"No," said Hellen with strange confidence she didn't normally have. Remembering what she had learned about the owner from the papers she had found in the library, the papers she still had on her in her dress pocket. Why, she had even seen his picture! "The owner is a man named Horace Derwent, he has a funny little mustache and silly glasses, and he was quite upset with you!"

This made Mr. Braddock stop counting. He put down the key he was holding in his hand and terror spread across his face as he looked down from behind the desk at Hellen and Teddy. "What did you say?"

"I said that Mr. Derwent told us himself that when he opened this hotel it was the showplace of the world, and that you've let it become this joyless and cold place." Hellen didn't like fibbing but found that she was rather good at it.

By now, poor Mr. Braddock was out from behind the desk and kneeling to meet Hellen and Teddy's eye level.

"Where did this happen? Where did you talk to Mr. Derwent!?" Mr. Braddock asked, he was visibly shaken, and his eyes darted around as if half expecting the owner of the hotel to jump out from behind one of the sofas in the lobby and yell '*Surprise!*'

Hellen could tell she had picked the right lie; Mr. B was shaking.

"He wanted to see you in the library. He's expecting you," Hellen said.

Mr. Braddock didn't hesitate, he took off at a brisk pace towards the library.

Teddy and Hellen looked over and saw that this left his box of keys unattended. But the box was still too high for them to reach.

"Hurry, we don't have a lot of time!" Hellen nodded to Teddy as they tied the twine tightly around the U-shaped magnet.

Hellen launched her little magnet on a rope towards the small metal box that lay on the counter.

She missed. Pulling the rope back quickly she wound it around her wrist as she reeled it back in.

Teddy was peeking around the corner, on lookout duty. The coast was clear and she nodded to Hellen.

Hellen spun the magnet around and around, like a manic magnet windmill and launched it towards the metal box. This time, the magnet latched on, but the box was heavy with keys and Hellen couldn't pull the box off the counter.

"Teddy, I need help," Hellen pulled on the rope with all her might, but the box only moved an inch.

Teddy was still keeping watch, the library wasn't that far from the lobby, and she could see the doorway that led to it on the far, far end of the main floor. Mr. Braddock would be back any moment and figure out that he had been tricked! Teddy knew that life was dumb sometimes, and so she had a good feeling that the moment she turned away from her post to help Hellen was the moment Mr. B would head out of the library and back towards the lobby desk. It was almost as if her starring at the library door was what was keeping him from coming back.

"Teddy!" Hellen yelled out for her sister again.

Teddy hesitated and then, resigned to what she knew was the dumb play. She rushed over to her sister and helped her yank at the long twine rope. They leaned into it and pulled with all their might, and the box moved all the way to the end of the desk, until it stopped, anchoring itself against a small rise in the marble countertop, causing the magnet to pop off the box.

The Grady sisters fell over on their butts and back a few feet from the lobby desk.

Teddy ran back to her post for a moment to check, and sure enough, Mr. Braddock, looking more worried than annoyed, was exiting the library and looking around, as if making one final check that the owner wasn't there before storming back to deal with the girls.

When Teddy ran back towards Hellen, Hellen was winding the twine again and preparing to launch the magnet.

"There's no time for this!" Teddy whined.

She crouched down to make herself into a little table and turned to Hellen.

"Get on top of me!" Teddy said.

"What? No. Are you crazy, I'll crush you!" Hellen gave her sister a strange look.

Teddy insisted, "I'm technically a little bigger than you, you old-face dummy, not get on my back and grab that box! We don't have time!"

Hellen sighed and ran towards her sister. She jumped on her sister's back and was able to reach the top of the concierge counter and grab the heavy box of keys.

"Hurry!" said Hellen, "We need to get to the elevator before Mr. Braddock sees us!"

Teddy ran ahead of Hellen, who was struggling to run with the heavy key-filled box, and pressed the elevator call button. And pressed it again and again and again until the door opened.

"You know you only have to press that button once. More pushes doesn't make me go any faster!" Otis smiled his sad smile as both girls rushed into the elevator.

"What you got there Hellen?" ssked a curious Otis.

"None of your goddamn business, Otis." said Teddy and Hellen at the same time.

And so the girls managed to sneak up into their own room without being spotted by their mother.

"She must be out looking for us," worried Hellen out loud.

But they didn't slow down, not wanting to worry about their mother right at that moment.

Hellen rushed into their room, dragging the heavy metal box behind her with the magnet, like a boxy dog on a leash. She dumped all the keys onto her bed and began going through them one by one. Teddy right behind her.

To Mr. Braddock's credit, he had properly labeled each and every key with a paper that told you which door-lock was its pair, and after carefully examining each key, Hellen realized that indeed the key to the attic was *not* in Mr. Braddock's box.

"This is ridiculous, we should have done this the other way around," Hellen sighed angrily. "We should have figured out if the key was in here to begin with, then we could have avoided this whole thing! And the worst part is we have no idea where the key could be, let alone the door to the attic! This is hopeless! We're no closer to understanding what's going on or who the little boy is than we were this morning! Today has been a terrible day and huge waste of our time!"

"Hey," Teddy said "Why don't we climb around on things to help clear our heads. Maybe we can get an idea if we're higher up."

"I don't feel like climbing," said Hellen, pouting.

"Come on, you big dummy, everyone loves climbing. Here, let's see if we can't find that secret attic door." Teddy was only saying this to make Hellen feel better, and Hellen only looked up to make Teddy feel better, but by looking up at the ceiling they actually saw something.

"Hmm, Teddy, do you see that?"

Teddy looked up and squinted her eyes. "I think so?"

"It looks like a little square in the middle of the ceiling. Like the lid of a box. Do you see it?"

"You mean that little square?"

"Yes, obviously. Do you think that could be the door?" They both looked at it, trying to see it clearly, but it was dark outside, and the lights were dim on the tippy top floor of the hotel.

"It doesn't seem to have a keyhole," said Teddy looking at the square.

"Maybe," Hellen said, as Teddy climbed one of the dressers in the room to get a better look, "it doesn't need a keyhole. Maybe the reason we haven't found the key is because there is no key. Remember, Sally said her skeleton key wouldn't work on that door, but a skeleton key is supposed to work on every door."

"Hellen, that's brilliant!" Teddy exclaimed from atop the dresser.

"We know from the blueprint that the attic is right above our room. And this hallway is right outside our door. So maybe that little square is an unlocked attic!" As Hellen said this, she became more and more convinced that this was true.

"But there is no way to reach it." Teddy frowned, straining to touch the ceiling from the top of the dresser. "It's no use."

"I have an idea." Hellen whistled and waited. As if on cue, Teddy's spiders all crawled up to Hellen and Teddy.

"Hey, how'd you learn to do that!?" Teddy said, quite impressed with her sister.

"I learned to listen to them, and when you listen

to someone they listen back." Maïa the spider nuzzled herself into Hellen's neck before jumping off her neck and onto Teddy's head. Teddy giggled as all her pet spiders crawled up her arms and legs. They were all there. All except Rose. "She must still be exploring!" Teddy said.

Hellen asked the spiders politely if they could call out to Rose so she could report what she'd learned. Teddy was overjoyed that Hellen was getting along with her pets. The spiders rubbed their legs together, like crickets, and it made a very soft *swishing* sound, too soft for the girls to hear but loud enough for Rose to poke her head out from a crack in the ceiling above.

"Oh hey, you're back," Rose said and lowered herself down on her web. "Good, there is some strange messed up beeswax going on up here. You should take a look."

"How are we going to get up there?" Hellen asked.

"Leave that to us," said Rose with a wink of half her spider eyes, she nodded at Bacon, Ghostpepper, Kingsley, Heddy, Mellick, Snow, Maïa, Buckle and Pugsley.

"Come on gang," she said to her fellow spiders.

The rest of the spiders joined Rose on her climb back up the wall and disappeared into cracks in the ceiling. Then all together and at once they came down from the little square above the girls, merging their webs and forming a strong line of webby rope that led from the panel to the young ghost sisters. Hellen pulled on it and the panel opened up, revealing a set of stairs that unfolded to the ground and lead up to the hidden attic door.

"Oh shit," Teddy whispered to Hellen, "Pugsley says we're about to lose our tits."

CHAPTER
SEVENTEEN

The girls monkey-barred their way up the folding stairs and crawled into the entrance of the attic, which Hellen noticed was not nearly as impressive as the rest of The Overlook. It was small and cramped, full of old blankets and towels, and quite frankly, very underwhelming for a hotel's brain. There really wasn't anything to lose your tits over and now Teddy thought that Pugsley has said that just to be cool. But then that's when they felt it, a strong energy coming from deeper inside the small, cramped space, the smell of mildew and mothballs stinging their little noses.

The attic stretched across the entire top floor of The Overlook, but it was a tight fit, more like a crawl space than an attic. Luckily the girls were small enough to easily shimmy around. Hellen led the way and crawled across the floorboards towards the pulsing energy. There were small vents in the floor through which they could see down into some of the rooms, but the rooms looked different from the attic, as if the vents were lenses covered in Vaseline, giving the images below a kind of shine.

"Over here," Rose said, crawling alongside the sisters, "this is where it's coming from."

The girls shimmied over to where Rose was and peeked down through one of the grates. The girls saw sped-up images, blurry and overlapping, of the many ghosts and guests of the hotel.

"This," Rose said "is where I think most of The Overlook's memories are. Even the memories that haven't happened yet."

"How does that even make sense?" Hellen asked.

"Time is not linear, nor does it unfold in a predictable way at The Overlook," Rose whispered to the girls as they all peeked through the vent. "I've started to realize that everything here sort of happens at once, causing time to collapse and become meaningless."

"You've got one strange little spider there, Teddy," said Hellen.

"Don't I know it." Teddy winked at Rose, who closed half of her eight eyes to wink back.

They looked down and saw images of Darla and Roger getting ready for a party, but Roger was not in his usual dog suit, he was dressed like a bear, and they look a lot less dead. They saw Mr. Duke working away furiously at his typewriter back when he could type more than the same sentence over and over, he actually looked happy. They saw Lloyd the doorman, but he wasn't a doorman, he was a bartender now, still a ghost, but he was getting ready for a night of work making martinis. The room changed patterns and layouts, almost as if it was a picture flip book but with hundreds of totally different images, not just hundreds of the same image moving slightly. *This is what dreams must look like from the inside of your brain*, Hellen thought, *like a million different movies happening at once and in an instant.*

Her Mommy had told them both when they were younger how a person usually has many dreams in the night, but they hardly ever remember all of them. And sometimes when a dream is particularly strange, it's usually because we are remembering a jumbled-up combination of bits from many different dreams and nightmares. That's what this looked like to Hellen, like the inside of The Overlook's dreams, its memories and its nightmares, all jumbled up. Everything the hotel has ever seen, will see and *might* see.

"Look," Hellen said, "There's the little boy! There's Danny! He's with his whole family."

Hellen looked at him excitedly through the vent.

There he was, with his father and mother. Hellen watched as flashes and moments of the little boy and his family played out below them like a silent movie: *The little boy and his mother playing, his dad writing something on a typewriter just like the one Mr. Duke has, Danny's dad checking on the boiler, Danny and his mom laughing and singing.* They seemed like a happy family.

"But we would know if a family like this had stayed in the hotel," said Teddy. "Wouldn't we?"

"Maybe this just hasn't happened yet, Teddy. Maybe this is an important thing, this family coming here, and that's why The Overlook is dreaming about it."

They kept looking down through the vent, the flurry of images and scenes rushing by below them like a river of old home videos.

There was the little boy standing in front of the model of The Overlook by the playground, Miss Carla being pushed along in her wheelchair, Roger growling like a dog/bear, Cook making a giant cake for the Hotel's opening night, Mr. Braddock tap dancing, Danny eating chocolate-chip cookies and laughing.

Hellen was getting excited as she spoke, "Look! There's all these memories of people who died here, but there are also things that haven't happened yet. Like Lloyd not being a doorman anymore, and Danny's dad! What if this is something that's *going* to happen. Maybe even soon!" She was smiling so much her face was starting to hurt, "And that means the boy will come for real. If that's true, then maybe he can stay here with us."

"You mean become a ghost?" Teddy asked.

"I mean yes, he would have to become a ghost. But look at that family. Doesn't it look like they are having fun here? Wouldn't it be great to have them living here in the hotel? To have new people to play with?"

"Yeah," smiled Teddy, "I admit it'd be fun to have another kid around. But you'd have to convince the parents to want to stay in this crazyshit hotel. Most people don't like living in hotels, and The Overlook isn't exactly The Plaza and we're not exactly a family of Eloises," Teddy pointed out.

"It sure isn't, but it is a very interesting place with very interesting people. We just need to make them see that! Look, I've collected all these articles from the library, and I'm sure everyone else in the hotel has things we could use. I could put them all in my scrapbook, the one that mom gave me. We could use some of Mr. Duke's novel!" Hellen was getting excited, "This hotel is full of history, and the ghosts all have their own stories, if we collected them all in my scrapbook and put it somewhere so that the family finds it, then they'd see what a great place this is to live!"

"But how do we make sure they become ghosts? It's very rare that alive guests ever even see us," Teddy asked her older sister.

"You said time works differently here, that it's all just kind of happening at once?" Hellen asked Rose.

"Well, it's more nuanced and complicated, with a lot of exceptions, but essentially, yes. Kind of."

"Right," Hellen said as she dug into the large pouch pocket in the front of her dress and pulled out the ornate invitation she had found in the library. "I just got an idea. Come on Teddy!"

They shimmy-crawled back through the cramped and narrow jungle gym that was the attic, until they were back at the entrance and looking down the rickety ladder that led back to their room.

They were laughing excitedly and talking over each other and so they didn't hear Rose the spider cough out a warning, nor did they hear the frustrated sigh of their mother, who waited for them, arms crossed and anger boiling, at the bottom of the rickety ladder.

CHAPTER
EIGHTEEN

There are few things in this world that are scarier than an angry mother. Yes, I know that there are mothers out there who are truly and actually evil, and have done monstrous things to their children, and those are the truly terrifying mothers. But there is a different kind of terror that comes from the fear of a mother who loves you, and whose mission in life is to make sure you are safe and protected. This brand of mother-anger comes from a place of instinct so deep that the rage is pure and justified and has the force of a thousand bears. Fact is, with one silent glare and rigid postured stance, a mother can stop a heart, or in this case, bust two little ghosts.

Mrs. Grady was not a woman who enjoyed breaking her routine, a routine composed mostly of watching over her children and taking baths. It was very rare that she raised her voice, but when she did, it put the fear into Hellen and Teddy.

They hated seeing their mommy get mad. But worse than that, so much worse, was when she would get so mad at them that she *wouldn't* shout. Wouldn't raise her voice, or a hand, or so much as raise the one good eyebrow she had, the one that hadn't been blown off by the blast from daddy's shotgun. No. She would just say, "Go to bed." Stoic and calm, and with the dispassionate emptiness you use when talking to a stranger.

They knew that when she said, '*Go to bed,*' and not '*It's bedtime,*' they were in trouble. There would be no bedtime story. No goodnight kiss. Just those three words. *Go. To. Bed.* Said in that empty way. *Go to bed*, was terrifying to the little Grady sisters. Because with each dispassionate word, they felt their mommy love them a little less.

And Hellen knew that look. The look that meant those words were coming. And Hellen recognized that look on what was left of her mother's face, the side which hadn't been caved in by a shotgun bullet.

Their mother stood by the bottom rung of the ladder to the attic, waiting for them to get down so she could say it. However, Teddy and Hellen just stayed there, halfway up and halfway down, that rickety ladder to the attic.

"Get down here right now. You two are in a lot of trouble," Mommy said.

But the sisters didn't budge.

"Don't move," Teddy whispered to Hellen. "She can't see us if we don't move."

"You're thinking of dinosaurs."

"No, I'm not."

"Girls, you disobeyed me, and you broke the rules. Get down here. Now." Her voice was calm, measured. Like she knew if she got too mad too quickly, they would scamper back up into the attic and she did not feel like crawling around up there, especially since she was wearing a bathrobe.

"You think if we stay up here, she'll get tired of being mad?" Teddy asked her older sister.

"That's the only plan I got." Hellen said as they looked down at their mother. Her one good eye glowing like the lit end of a cigarette.

Mrs. Grady looked up at her daughters and sighed. It had been a long day.

Linnea Grady had always been a creature of habit. She had formed a kind of security-blanket relationship with predictability ever since she was a child, and she loved things kept boring, simple and safe.

"For most living things on this planet," she would say, "every day of their lives is only about one thing: survival. They don't have the luxury to be bored. If you can live a boring life, you're living a blessed life."

When she was six years old her father asked her what kind of pet she wanted for her birthday, she was growing up, he explained, and she was ready for responsibilities. She had asked her father for an ant farm.

He got her a puppy. But didn't want a puppy. Puppies are too unpredictable. At first it was okay, the puppy was cute and had big dumb floppy ears. It had a lot of energy, which Linnea was wary of, but she noticed that all the puppy did was eat, sleep, go to the bathroom and run. It was boring. She was happy.

But one day the puppy got sick, got into some brownie mix that Linnea's mom had thrown away, and the little puppy shot vomit and shit out each end, making a huge mess.

Since this was a pet meant to teach the young Linnea responsibilities, it was her job to clean after the dog. She hated how it made her feel when the puppy got sick, hated how gross it was that she was responsible for cleaning up its mess, the dog shit and piss and vomit was everywhere! She was mad that she didn't get the ant farm she wanted—ant farms are easy, predictable, safe.

So, the next day, she grabbed some glass from the

garage where her dad kept his tools and work stuff, she went to the sandbox in her backyard, and she built herself an ant farm for the puppy.

Trapping the puppy between the sandbox and the glass.

Even though the puppy died, there was something so calming to her with how predictably the whole thing had played out.

At nineteen, she met Delbert. He was a boring man. A nervous and shy man. Illiterate but faithful, and good at small, practical jobs. She could tell he'd never been with a woman before, that he would be grateful.

He had a summer job looking after horse stables for a rich country club, would come home smelling of horse shit every night. His frog-like eyes, watering from the intense smell of manure that stung his nostrils every day. She felt secure knowing other women wouldn't dare to touch him because of the stench, and she loved that.

As for the winters, he would watch over an old hotel that would close for the season, out in the middle of God-knows-where, Colorado. Their lives were a rut of routine that was exactly what Linnea had always wanted.

The arrival of two daughters, while that wasn't what one would call boring, wasn't all that novel or interesting. Both pregnancies went along without major incident and both girls were born on their exact due date.

Hellen, named after Hellen of Troy, and Theodora, after a Roman empress.

Although there were lots of unknowns with having children, Linnea had learned her lesson from the puppy incident and found other ways to make sure her daughters lived a life of boring predictability.

She homeschooled them both, for one, and she bought them the same outfits, so she never had to stress about their clothing.

And yes, she had failed to provide them shelter and safety when Delbert lost his mind that night, but it wasn't all her fault.

The hotel, she thought, always seemed to get its way. And that constant truth seemed to calm her and make her feel less guilt. An old hotel with a nonsense impossible architecture and a history of death and murder, why this was, after all, the most predictable place for a ghost to be.

So, she carved out a good routine for herself and her girls once they realized that they weren't going anywhere, and The Overlook would be their new perpetual home.

She had spoken to Delbert, and he had agreed, for the sake of keeping the peace, that he would not be around the hotel much during the day.

"I'll leave you and the girls alone, stay away from them and ensure that they never accidentally stumble upon me during their little hotel adventures—but only during the day. Once that sun sets, they're fair game, as long as they're out of their room. If they're roaming about when it's dark out, well then, I'll get to see my little girls, say I'm sorry and, bury the hatchet so to speak."

She didn't smile.

"Come on, you used to love my dad jokes," Delbert teased.

"It's a deal. I keep them in their room once the sun goes down and you stay the fuck away from us during the day."

"That's what I said."

"Well then, that's all there is to talk about," she said and got up to leave the kitchen.

"Lin, there's one more thing you might like to know..." Delbert said.

But when he turned to face her, she was gone.

She always did like to keep things simple and clean. The deal was done, and she clearly didn't need to hear another word come out of that son of a bitch's mouth.

So now, despite the bullet hole in her head and her two dead daughters, she had found a good routine that made her once again feel boring, predictable and safe.

Every morning she would wake up Teddy and Hellen and send them off to eat their breakfast, allowing them the day to play and explore while she went down to check the boiler, something her husband was supposed to do, but taking over that duty had been part of their deal. He stayed away during the day, she took over his chores, at least until a new caretaker came up for the winter.

After the boiler room, she would feed Teddy's

spiders. Teddy didn't even know she did this, but she liked the stability of gathering flies and dropping them into the webs. That fact that there were an even ten of them also gave her comfort. She made the beds for the girls, then she would walk around the hotel, making sure Delbert was keeping his promise and staying out of sight.

After her rounds, she usually went down to her suite, room 217, to get her bath ready. The water on the second floor would come out scalding hot, and once you fill the tub you have to wait about two hours until you can get in without blistering. However, it's not long before the hot water runs out and turns to a useless tepid temperature that might as well be horse spit. So, she has to prepare her bath before she tucks the girls in for bedtime, and time it out so that after she tells them their bedtime story she can go to her room and into a perfect bath.

It has to be timed just right because old lady Massey in room 237 uses up all the hot water. All that bitch does all day is take baths. Linnea is pretty certain that the reason the whole floor only gets about 40 minutes of hot water a day is because of the greedy bath pig in 237.

But she'd gotten the timing down to a science, and as long as everyone was on time, it would not affect her sacred routine.

But today, today had been different, because when the winter sun set, and the time of day had come when her daughters should have been in their rooms, waiting for their mother to tell them a story and put them to bed, they were not.

The first reaction that went through Linnea was panic. For someone so reliant on routine, a break from it was like an earthquake. She frantically checked under the beds, in the closets, anywhere her little ones might be hiding.

Her nerves were rising, it was after dark, and she couldn't find them! If she still had a pulse, she'd be hearing the loud thump of blood pumping in her ears, and little else.

The panic was spreading through her system like a drug, tightening its grip on her stomach and pulling at the muscles in her back, twisting them like a knot.

She felt the aggressive tug at her throat of a dry heave, like a fishing hook in her lungs tugging upward.

Linnea was prone to paranoia, and one could argue, that as a mother who got shot in the face and whose daughters were hacked to death by the man she trusted, it was justifiable.

Even though her daughters were ghosts, they could

still feel pain and fear, could still get hurt. This hotel had proven many times over that no one, not even the dead, were truly safe.

She needed to calm herself down, to snap herself out of this upcoming panic attack. She tied her bathrobe shut tightly around her waist, took a deep breath and dug her fingernails into her bulletwound.

Red hot pain seared through her. She scratched and pinched at the exposed nerves and raw face meat in the hole that would never heal.

A long stream of tears poured down her one good eye. The sharp agony brought her back to the moment and churned the panic into dull, predictable pain.

She knew the boring thing to say when someone or something is missing is: 'it's always in the last place you look,' which is another way of saying, 'it's most likely either in the least likely place, or the place you'd least like it to be."

Predicting her own bad luck, Linnea knew that this probably meant that she'd have to start with the last place she'd want to find her daughters.

CHAPTER
NINETEEN

innea Grady stood in front of the big double doors that lead to The Colorado Lounge, the hotel's large ballroom that sat opposite the elevators and behind the lobby. The guests and staff called it The Gold Room because of the color scheme and the actual golden sconces and table legs, the bright golden carpet that hugged the floor like a giant lion-skinned snake. As she walked through the double doors, the Colorado Lounge expanded. Emptiness and silence made it seem all the bigger, too big to exist inside The Overlook.

Linnea had never been to one of the fabled parties that had been thrown there, nor did she think she would have particularly been comfortable had she attended one. But all the same, she let herself imagine the room filled with elegance and class, with jazz musicians and glasses of pink champagne cluttering her view, letting herself be distracted for just a moment before refocusing on the task at hand.

She walked towards the long bar, by the men's room, which was designed to be a polished twin to the long reception desk in the lobby. She looked up, half expecting to see a bartender waiting to serve her a drink, but the room was empty, and the bar was covered in a warren of dust-bunnies.

Linnea slipped through the small entry to the bathroom where a red rug with a decorative black and red diamond pattern welcomed her. She turned right and through a second door, tuned right again and through a random and totally unnecessary third door, which took her inside the bathroom and also, according to a bird's eye view of the situation, would simultaneously place her back at the bar in the ballroom. As if she had made a small circle back to where she started, but instead had ended up in the men's room.

There was newspaper all over the floor, and Delbert was in the back of the room painting the walls bright red. Covering up the original midnight blue, with this new hellish and disorienting shade.

"I know what you're thinking," said Delbert casually, without looking up from his work. He was using a flat paintbrush and coating the walls with even strokes, "Too red, right? I said the same thing. But this is what Management wants."

There was something about the way he was working, doing menial labor and having a folksy conversation with her, that was comforting, and this bothered her.

"I'm not here to talk about the color of the walls, although my god, it looks like the inside of a migraine in here, no Delbert, I came down here to talk about our girls."

Delbert's hands were covered in red paint, and he made a little happy face on the wall with his finger before covering it up with a fresh coat. "What about them?" He asked, still not looking at her.

"I can't find them. Just wanted to make sure you didn't..."

"Didn't what?" He said, finally looking up from his work to stare at the face of his wife. "Didn't teach those girls a lesson? Why? Those little hellions getting in trouble again? Playing with matches again?"

He was smiling when he said this, almost suppressing a laugh.

"You think this is a fucking joke?" Linnea said through gritted teeth.

"Oh, you know me, darlin', I wasn't much for thinking. I let my daddy do the thinking for me 'fore I met you, and you did most of the thinking for me when we were together. This place, this wonderful hotel, took over for you when we got here. Told me what to do, when to do it. I'm not a thinking man, Lin, never was. Oh, I'm a good man for hard labor, I can paint you a wall, push a button, flip a switch. Speaking of—"

"Yes," she said, "I always remember the boiler."

"That's good. That's what it wants. It wants us to be paying attention, it wants us to help it."

"Delbert, have you seen the girls? Just answer the question."

"No darlin', I told you I wouldn't go seekin' them out, and a promise is a promise. Huh, remember that book? *A Promise is a Promise*. That was by that fella Bobby Munsch? Was that even published when we were alive?"

He smiled as he rubbed his eyes with the back of his hand, careful to not get paint on his face, "Time is real strange here ain't it? Like everything in the world kinda all happenin'."

He winked at her, and she noticed herself in the bathroom mirrors, the ones over the sinks and the freshly painted bright-red counters they rested on.

She was no longer in her Overlook bathrobe. She was in her wedding dress. A slim and modest white dress with a flapper hat that functioned as a veil.

She brought her hand up to her face. It was whole. The bullet wound, gone.

She fought hard to keep herself from crying, from showing any emotion.

Delbert came up behind her, putting a hand on her ass, holding her tightly in place while smearing her dress with a red handprint.

"This is how I remember you, Lin. This is how I always see you."

She looked away, not wanting to forget the hate she had for this man, but he knew how to get her defenses down. Like he said, he was good at pushing buttons. She let herself ease up as he turned her face back toward the mirror, and she saw herself again, but this time the bullet hole had returned, and Delbert held her face in place, smearing red paint on her cheeks, and laughed.

She pushed him away and stormed out of the bathroom. He was cruel, but she knew he hadn't taken the girls. He would have been too proud of that not to brag about it.

She left the bathroom, wiping away at the paint on her cheeks and catching a glimpse of herself, still in her modest wedding dress. On the back of her dress was a red palm print. The stain made her incredibly self-conscious, as she noticed what had just moments ago been a deserted ballroom was now full of people. A roaring 20s themed party was in full swing and people all around her were dancing, eating and having stimulating conversations.

She saw the back of the dress on the reflection of the shiny black marble on the base of the bar and then looked out at the party. People didn't seem to be paying any attention to her. She furrowed her brow and even though she was sure this moment was a hotel memory and not an impromptu ghost gathering, she was still mortified at the thought that someone would notice her stained dress.

She needed to get out of there, but true to her nature, did not want to cause a scene or draw any unwanted attention.

She kept a brisk pace, and walked as casually as she could, passed elegantly dressed men and women, towards the entrance which was blocked by a seemingly infinite row of diners seated at ornate, candlelit tables. She walked by a bald man covered in confetti who smiled at her and raised his glass of champagne, she kept her head down and walked past a man who didn't quite fit in there either, while everyone at the party was wearing formal wear, this man was in jeans and a casual wine-colored jacket.

He seemed so out of place that she was sure it must mean something, but she also knew that this was the kind of thing the hotel did, try to distract her, trap her. Linnea thought it best to just get out of there as fast as she could. She needed to find her daughters. The fact that they weren't with Delbert was a relief, but also made that familiar panic bubble back up. If they weren't here, then where could they be?

When Linnea left the Colorado Lounge the hotel quieted down, she was back to wearing her untainted and pristine white bathrobe, and the stench of red paint and cheap cigarettes that lingered from Delbert had evaporated. She collected herself and set out to scour the hotel in search of Hellen and Teddy. But they weren't at the playground or the hedge maze, where Mrs. Grady noticed two topiary animals, not sure of what they used to be, in pieces on the ground. She checked the library and saw all these maps strewn around the floor, but no daughters. She checked the kitchen, the impossible window, the room with the best furniture for climbing, but she came up empty. This hotel was big but not infinite - there were only so many places the girls could be.

After making the rounds one last time, Linnea decided to end her search where she began it, knowing her luck, the girls had snuck back into their room while she was out looking for them, and if that were true then she'd punish them both harder than she ever had for making her worry.

She took the stairs up to the tippy top floor, she didn't like getting into the elevator with that balloon of a man, and walked into Hellen and Teddy's room, ready to start yelling at them, but they weren't there, but before she could react with more of her trademark panic, she heard a loud creak of old hinges and the singular sound of a rickety ladder being unfolded as it lowered itself from attic door to bedroom floor.

Teddy and Hellen hadn't moved for what seemed like a couple of eternities. They stood frozen on the steps of the ladder unsure of exactly what to do. Just waiting the situation out. "What's your read on Mom?" Teddy whispered to Hellen.

"Can't really tell. It's like I think she looks relieved to see us, but that could also be a trap."

"Right, right. Rose, what's your take?" Teddy whispered to her spider co-parent.

"I'm quite tired at the moment, Teddy. I think we're all just a little tired." She gave Teddy a little spider kiss and nodded at the other spiders who were all up in the attic, peeking out from the edge of the opening.

"You two can take it from here," and with that Rose, Barnaby and the others used their webbing to gently lower themselves down to their nests below.

"Well, that's bullshit," whispered Hellen. "They're all in until the first sign of trouble and then they bail?

What gives with your spiders Teddy?"

Teddy just shrugged, "Eh, that's the spider way I guess."

They looked down at their mother and tried to figure out from her expression what she was thinking. If they had the kind of power some people have, where they can peek into other people's thoughts, they would have been able to tell that Linnea Grady was relieved, and that all she wanted to do was hug her little blackbirds tight. But she also wanted them to learn a lesson, to know that disappearing and breaking routine was absolutely not allowed! If they could read her mind, they would know that she was trying very hard to stand her ground and not let the anger get drowned out by the relief.

But they couldn't read minds, and so Hellen asked her mother "Are you mad at us?" with Teddy saying it at the same time.

Mrs. Linnea Grady looked at her daughters, the daughters she once failed to protect and the daughters she had sworn to never again put in harm's way, standing awkwardly on the ladder, like porcelain figurines balanced on the branch of an old tree, and the anger just melted away.

"I'm not mad." The words came out soft and comforting, betraying her lesson-teaching intent, "But if I were still alive, I'd have been worried sick! Now, what on earth have you two been up to?"

Hellen and Teddy told their mother all about their adventures that day. How it all started when Hellen saw a little boy who wasn't there.

"It's true mom," Teddy told her mother, "Hellen and I saw him with our own eyes. Only it wasn't him it was just a memory that hasn't happened yet."

"Yes, the hotel does tend to have strange visions sometimes," she remembered the ballroom full of people she had walked through only hours before.

"Well, we were up in the attic, and we saw a whole bunch of things!" Hellen was so excited that the words were all getting stuck in her mouth. "Now we just have to go and talk to the Manager."

But this stopped their mother. Her smile dropped and she looked at them with concern. "How do you know about the Manager?"

"Hellen was so smart, she figured it all out. She figured the way to talk to the Manager so we can ask them to help us with Danny."

"Well, Teddy was so brave tonight mom. She was able to fight a hedge lion and shark! And her spiders were so resourceful!" Hellen said and Teddy beamed as her sister complimented her.

"I am so proud of my little blackbirds," their mother smiled. "Now, Hellen, what is it you need to speak to the Manager about?"

"I need to talk to them about something important. A favor. I even have an idea for a gift."

Hellen took out all the clippings and things she had collected in the library and from cook, including the engraved invitation to the hotel's grand opening.

"I collected all this stuff about the hotel. I was thinking we could put it in my scrapbook, the one you gave me for my birthday."

"That's a great idea, let's all work on it together."

With Hellen placing and Mom gluing and Teddy jumping up and down on the bed, cheering them on, they got the work done in no time at all.

When it was all done Mom gave Hellen and Teddy permission to go to the Gold Room and talk to the Manager. But to come back to bed right after that, and in the meantime, Mom would be able to enjoy her nice hot bath.

Hellen held the finished scrapbook. Each page was now full of old newspaper clippings about the hotel, articles and photos of its former owner, Horace Derwent, and drawings from Hellen and Teddy. They'd stuck all the clippings about the various deaths at the hotel that they got from Cook inside there too. All of The Overlook's history—both good and bad— was crammed inside the scrapbook! Hellen was so proud of this idea. There was enough stuff in it to show the new family that was coming what a great and interesting place The Overlook was, and hopefully this would be enough to make Danny and his family excited to stay.

CHAPTER
TWENTY

The girls stood in front of the large ornate double-doors that opened into the grand and expansive golden ballroom.

"Okay, focus on going to the grand opening of the hotel," Teddy told Hellen, "picture we are already there, and then open your eyes."

Teddy closed her eyes and whispered to herself, "I wish I was at the opening gala!"

When she opened her eyes, Hellen was just looking at her like Teddy had just tried to recreate a meal by eating a fart.

She rolled her eyes.

"Teddy, this isn't the wizard of Oz. We need to use the invitation."

Hellen opened up her scrapbook and took the

invitation from the first page and looked at it.

It was a rich and creamy shade of white, like a marshmallow egg, the paper had a raised engraving of the hotel, with yellow paint in each window, showing a hotel alive with light, apparently already full before it even opened. The lawn and playground in the image on the invitation were decorated with glowing paper lanterns. It looked almost as though you could step right into it, The Overlook Hotel as it had existed more than thirty years ago.

Hellen read the invitation out loud to the large ornate doors that lead to the ballroom, as if she were reciting a password to a hidden speakeasy.

"Horace M. Derwent requests the pleasure of your company at a masked ball to celebrate the grand opening of The Overlook Hotel. August 29, 1945"

Hellen held her breath, waiting for something to happen.

"RSVP Dinner at eight!" Teddy added, reading the last line of the invite.

The girls looked at each other and grabbed onto the door handles and leaned backwards, using their full body weight to pull open the large doors.

When they peeked inside, it was full of music and hotel guests, of balloons and bottles and confetti poppers!

In the ballroom, there was a decade's worth of business conventions taking place at the same time, and in the dining room, seventy years of meals were being served simultaneously and there was steady chatter and cigarette smoke coming from the Colorado Lounge.

The girls held hands and walked into the mad rush of laughter and music all competing with the hundreds of loud and boisterous conversations that were happening at once.

They passed by a man, bald shiny head above his eyebrows and a small glass of golden-brown drink in his hands. Teddy thought it was dark apple juice, but Hellen recognized it as whisky, like their dad used to drink.

The bald man was smiling and had confetti splattered on his shoulders as if a clown took a bird-crap on him, his cheeks and nose were red, like he'd been playing outside in the snow.

"Great party, isn't it?" He said to the girls as they walked by him. "Have a drink, have a cigar!"

He handed them one of the cigars that Cook had told them about, A Cherry Rum Cigar.

"They are soaked in cherry-red rum. It turns 'em pink and makes them taste like candy!"

"Really Horace, they're children," said a voice from behind a small crowd of party goers.

"That's precisely the point I was making with the candy comment. That children will love them because of the cherry taste."

"Please Horace, you go entertain your guests. Let Us tend to this."

Horace shrugged and turned toward the next guest he could find.

"Great party, isn't it?" he said, as he was swept away into the ocean of people.

"Now, let's take a look at you two."

The crowd around the voice parted and Hellen and Teddy saw who it was that had taken a sudden interest in them.

Well, sort of. She was a woman, tall and elegant, like a human mink, dressed in a gorgeous shiny dress that twinkled here and there in subtle ways, *the sparkle of the ocean at night*, as she walked. There was an intensity to her, but also a calming confidence that made you feel somehow safe as well as petrified.

Hellen thought this was what a mouse must feel when it's caught in a staring contest with an owl.

The woman was wearing a mask so Hellen and Teddy couldn't see her face clearly.

"Hello Grady sisters," she said. "Welcome to the party."

With a wave of her gloved hand, the crowd around her dispersed and she took a seat on a small red ottoman that was next to a sofa, she patted the cushions of the sofa and gestured to Hellen and Teddy that they should take a seat.

Teddy jumped on the little sofa and started to balance on the arm rest, Hellen was more cautious and approached it slowly.

"Who are you?" Hellen asked the woman in the mask.

"Why, We are the Manager," she said in a hushed snake whisper, "and We hear you've been looking for Us."

She smiled.

Hellen stepped closer to the couch and the ottoman the woman was sitting on, trying to get a better look at her face. Although the mask only covered her eyes, it was hard to make out what she looked like underneath it. There was something sinister about this woman, but Hellen couldn't figure it out.

The closest thing she could compare it to was what her mother told her mermaids used to do with sailors lost at sea, lure them in with a sweet song and then drown them in the coldest oceans. The Manager seemed like a siren.

"Come now, Hellen, We're not going to bite," she said, as if reading Hellen's mind. "Now, you've come all this way, figured out how to get to the party. How *did* you end up in here anyway?"

"Hellen found the invitation!" Teddy laughed as she balanced precariously on the back of the sofa.

"That's right, I found this old invitation, I figured since time works all wonky here, I could use it to find you."

"And now you've found Us, little ones, so what is it you need?"

Hellen struggled to find the words, she hadn't really thought her plan out and now that she was faced with having to explain it, she couldn't figure out how to get it out. She held the scrapbook tight to her chest, all of a sudden very self-conscious about this whole thing. The woman in the mask bent down and smiled at her, it was a reassuring Cheshire smile.

"It's okay little one. You can tell Us."

"Well, you see," Hellen started, "it started when I saw a little boy in the hotel. A little boy who wasn't there."

"Ah yes," said the Manager, "we are aware of this. A family, the winter caretakers, a couple with a young son, they will be arriving soon."

"Yes!" Hellen and Teddy said excitedly.

"Teddy and I saw him earlier and then he disappeared. When we went into the attic, we saw all sorts of stuff about that family. We think there might be a way for us to convince the family to stay here, with us for forever and not just the winter."

The Manager sat back down on the ottoman and once again patted the couch cushion, inviting Hellen to sit. This time she did. The Manager just looked at the Grady sisters, and said nothing for a long while, as if sizing them up.

Hellen and Teddy stared back, uncharacteristically still, the sounds of adults having meaningless conversations and clinking glasses, like white noise in the background.

And then, like magic, the crowd disappeared and it was only The Manager and the Grady girls alone in the giant golden ballroom.

"We are very impressed with you," said the Manager with a smile. "There are many who have been here for much longer than you two have, and still haven't figured out how to find me. Much less how to access The Overlook's dreams. Yes, we are very aware of this little boy you saw Hellen, and we too would very much like him to stay here with Us. But it is not so easy. Children are the ones who shine the strongest but are also the hardest to harness."

"What are you talking about?" Teddy asked The Manager, "And what happened to the party?"

"What do you mean 'harness'?" Asked Hellen.

"It is difficult to explain. But let's just say that when we are born, we all have a certain amount of light inside us. Some have more than others. This light, it has a shine to it, and children - well their light shines the strongest."

"Do we have the light?" Teddy asked.

"Of course you did. That's why you can talk to spiders." Answered The Manager.

"So if you shine you can talk to spiders?!"

"Well, Teddy not always. That's just how it came out for you and your sister. For some kids it's reading minds, or starting fires with their thoughts, moving objects without touching them. It's all sorts of things really. But it's this shine that powers The Overlook.

When someone dies here, the hotel takes that light and uses it."

"Well that's perfect! If Danny has that shining light thing you want, and we want him to stay, then all we have to do is make sure he dies here, and everybody wins!" Hellen said excitedly.

"Like We were saying, it's not as simple as that. Children shine the strongest, but because of that they are protected by that energy. Adults are easier to control, *manipulate*, but their steam is weaker and less useful. In order to make someone want to harm a child, it requires a lot of energy on Our part. Steam we can't spare."

"Steam? I thought you said it was a shine," said Hellen.

"Shine, steam, *the force*, people call it all sorts of names, but we're talking about energy. Pure energy. And We mean pure in the sense that it's untainted and uncorrupted. The kind that tastes like cupcakes and could power a small town. The kind that keeps this hotel special and alive."

"If kids have the most steam, then how come there aren't more kids here?" Teddy asked again.

"You need the parents to want their child to stay here. But it's hard to do—your father, dear Gradys, was a simple man and was easy to manipulate, no offense, but someone smarter and more together than Delbert, will require more."

"But what if we all help out. It doesn't have to be just you doing it, what if all the ghosts at The Overlook helped! What if we all worked together to make the family stay here." Hellen said, not ready to let this go.

"Easier said than done, my darling. We're afraid the deceased guests at this hotel don't quite like Us. We being the cause most of them are trapped in here in the first place. However," The Manager looked at Hellen and Teddy's adorable matching outfits, their cute little faces, their heartbreaking quest for a new friend, who could say no to them? "If you two got everyone to help, that might work. We'd have to target the father, he's always the easier one to push over the edge. Make him obsessed with this place the way we did with your father."

"Hellen had a plan, tell her your plan Hell." Teddy nudged her sister.

Hellen held out the scrapbook and showed it to The Manager.

"Well, you see, I thought if we could make a collection of everything that made this hotel special and unique, the new family would want to stay here, so I gathered all these things about The Overlook and the ghosts who live here and put it in this book."

The Manager flipped through the pages of the scrapbook, admiring the collection of information that Hellen had managed to put together.

"We figured if we put it somewhere they are sure to find it, then it would be a good start." Hellen smiled, proud of her plan now that she was hearing it out loud for the first time.

"This is a magnificent idea!" The Manager was actually very impressed with them. "If you can convince the others to help Us, to help *you*, then this might work. If we all worked together, get the father obsessed with the hotel, exploit his weaknesses, get into his head…it's a long shot, but it might work."

The Manager was up on her feet, making a plan in her head and talking more to herself than to Hellen and Teddy.

"The new caretaker will have to check the boiler room. I know that because mommy has to do it every day. Maybe we can put the book in the boiler room, since we know he will have to go there!"

"Teddy, that's a perfect idea!" The Manager smiled, "Thank you girls, it has been so long since We've seen such a bright shine coming to the hotel with such a clear path on how to keep it here. You two are very special girls."

"So, if we convince everyone to help us make Danny's daddy go crazy, the way the hotel made our Dad go crazy, then Danny might be able to stay here with us? Forever and ever?" Teddy asked.

"That is Our hope." The Manager smiled. She got

up and started to walk towards a golden door by the bar that hadn't been there moments before.

"Do you really think this will work? Do you really think we can get them to stay?" Hellen called out.

The Manager turned back and winked at them as she disappeared through the strange golden door, "We'll just have to wait and see." And with that the Manager was gone. Hellen looked over at her sister.

"Was it me or did she seem super odd to you?"

"Oh yeah, total whackadoo. But she also seems like someone who can get shit done." Teddy jumped off the couch and looked up at Hellen.

"So what's the plan, Hell?"

"I think we go upstairs and get tucked in and get mom to tell us a bedtime story. We can figure out the next move tomorrow. All we have is time, you know. An eternity of time."

EPILOGUE

Every night before Hellen and Teddy go to sleep, their mother comes to visit them and tells them a bedtime story.

Their mother always starts the story the same way:

Once upon a time there were two little blackbirds that were the best of friends. They would fly around the sky and dig in the dirt for worms, they would laugh and sing and play games all day. They loved and looked out for each other, as good little blackbirds do.

They lived in a nest made out of an old wicker basket on the tippy top branch of an aspen tree that overlooked the garden. One day one little bird asked of her friend, 'would they still be able to play together, like they did now, even when they were old birds? Even when the winds became too much for them, could they still play together?'

But the other bird looked at her friend and shook her head sadly, she told the bird that even though they would play together now, that as time went by, they would fly in different directions, they would grow up and grow apart. Because that, unfortunately, is often how it works when we grow older.

But, said the first little bird, if we find the wishing rock, then we could wish to be friends forever and to never become old!

And so they set out to find the wishing rock.

And when the little blackbirds at last found it, they fluttered around in great excitement. They asked the rock to be able to remain young and be able to play together always and forever.

The rock heard their wish and knew it was pure, for young little blackbirds are always good of heart.

And it was then that the magical woodsman came out of the woods with his magic wand. He went to the little birds and whacked their little heads and wings with the magical stick.

Whack whack whack.

And just like that, the magic had been cast. The little birds would remain young and pure and never grow old. Now they could return to their nest to play forever and ever and ever.

"Mommy?" asked Hellen.

"Yes my dear?"

"The little birds, did they ever get more birds to play with?"

"Of course, my dears. Every time the magic woodsman hits a little bird with his magic wand, they become young forever."

"Tell it again please." Hellen and Teddy say.

And this time, when Teddy says the same words at the same time, Hellen doesn't mind.

ABOUT THE AUTHOR

Simon Oré Molina is an imaginary friend for hire and a lover of snacks, especially chips and cereal. In addition to watching cartoons, smoking on the porch, whittling flamingos, and listening to *They Might Be Giants* music, he makes films and writes books.

ABOUT THE ILLUSTRATOR

Roman Dirge is an American comic book writer, artist, and former magician. He is best known as the creator of the comic book series *Lenore, the Cute Little Dead Girl.*

www.ingramcontent.com/pod-product-compliance
Lightning Source LLC
Chambersburg PA
CBHW020327260626
47156CB00004B/1418